Exception to Murder

Exception to Murder

Anne Wingate

Walker and Company
New York

I want to dedicate this one to
Naomi Wingate,
a very special friend for many reasons.

Particular thanks are due my husband,
T. Russell Wingate,
who did so much of the work on this book
that he should be listed as coauthor.

First published in the United States of America in 1992
by Walker Publishing Company, Inc.

Published simultaneously in Canada by Thomas Allen & Son
Canada, Limited, Markham, Ontario

Library of Congress Cataloging-in-Publication Data
Exception to murder / Anne Wingate.
p. cm.
ISBN 0-8027-3203-8
I. Wingate. II. Title.
PS3573.I5316E93   1991
813' .54--dc20   91-29968
CIP

Printed in the United States of America
2 4 6 8 10 9 7 5 3 1

▽

Chapter 1

"I SUPPOSE THE FIRST question is, how are we going to get it out of there?" Chief Mark Shigata said, eyeing the body with somewhat more than the usual degree of uneasiness.

"I ain't volunteering," replied Al Quinn, whose promotion to captain had done nothing to increase his politeness. Shigata chuckled.

"But we better figure something out soon," Quinn added. "The park opens in half an hour."

"At least it's Thursday," Shigata said. "The kids'll be in school. So the crowd shouldn't be too big. We can put evidence tape around this area."

"Right," Quinn said. "And then station an army around the evidence tape to keep people away."

Shigata nodded. The Bayport, Texas, Police Department had several problems, one of which was its size—only eighteen sworn officers—and in a theme park it was only to be expected that people would tend to ignore a police line. "We may have to tell them not to open on time," he said, and turned his attention back to the alligator pit.

"Right," Quinn said. "Saying it is one thing. Getting Hobby to do it is another."

"So true, so true," Shigata agreed. The Reverend Clifford Hobby, television minister and owner of the theme park—or

1

rather, head of the religious (quasi-religious, Shigata was inclined to believe) organization that owned ArkPark—had not thus far shown any great tendency to cooperate with the police on anything, although he certainly wanted the police department to cooperate with him on things such as providing extra officers on demand to control traffic in the park. But, fortunately, the Reverend Clifford Hobby had not put in an appearance so far this morning; the body had been discovered, and reported to the police, by one of the residents of the Reverend Clifford Hobby's homeless shelter, who had been detailed along with several other residents to feed the animals.

The body seemed to be that of a late-middle-aged woman who probably, before the alligators had gotten to her, had been neatly dressed. But the alligators—whose presence in ArkPark rather puzzled Shigata anyway—had gotten to her at least ten hours ago, and what was left of the body, of the slightly rounded head with short, gray-brown hair and whatever color they had been eyes, of the sturdy torso and arms covered with a brown linen suit, of the legs and feet covered with nylon stockings and brown alligator pumps, was anything but neat.

Because the hands were totally gone, Shigata hoped she would be otherwise identifiable. What was left was scattered around the alligator pit; one leg had been dragged to the far end of the pit, near a large mound of wet grass, and the other was in the central pool. Two obviously well-fed alligators—presumably male and female, Shigata thought, as he was pretty sure alligators were ritually unclean animals and the park was trying, among other things, to reproduce the contents of Noah's Ark—were now dozing in the early morning sunshine.

Sergeant Steve Hansen, Ph.D., leaped lightly over the mortared stone retaining wall.

"What the hell do you think you're doing?" Shigata yelled. "Get out of there!"

"They're not hungry anymore," Hansen pointed out.

"What do you mean they're not—"

"If they were still hungry," Hansen said, "they'd have finished eating her." He moved toward the main portion of the body, then glanced around. "On second thought—"

He snatched a slightly chewed on brown alligator bag from the ground and leaped back over the wall as a large, hissing alligator began to move toward him.

"You were saying?" Shigata inquired politely.

"On second thought, maybe they are still hungry," Hansen said. "But at least I've got this." He dropped the bag on the picnic table that stood near the alligator pit. He glanced back toward the pit. "That one's probably a male," he commented.

"You're now an expert in sexing alligators?" Quinn inquired.

"No, but the females don't usually go over about nine feet, and that one's eleven feet if it's an inch."

"How do you know that?" Shigata asked.

"I read it somewhere," Hansen said, and then thought about it. "Actually I read it in World Book, come to think of it."

"Is there anything you *haven't* read somewhere?" Quinn asked.

"Lots of things," Hansen said, and leaned over the table to watch Shigata. "But the last five years I had plenty of reading time." That was true; it was within the last fifteen months that Hansen had been released from the state penitentiary at Huntsville, where he had gone after being convicted of a murder he did not commit.

Shigata, gingerly opening the handbag, didn't say anything about possible fingerprints on it. He doubted even the FBI laboratory could raise prints from rough-textured leather that had been chewed on by at least one alligator. But still, from force of habit, he nudged its contents out with the barrel of a pen rather than with his fingers. It was, he thought, unusually tidy inside, at least in comparison to most of the women's purses he had opened. An oxblood leather billfold-checkbook combination, snapped shut. A plastic-wrapped package of facial tissue. An oxblood leather cigarette pouch, with a pocket on the side containing a disposable lighter. A small daybook, also oxblood but, he thought, vinyl instead of leather. The only slightly incongruous item was a plastic sandwich bag containing a carved ivory bracelet and two carved ivory hairpins that couldn't possibly have been worn in the woman's short hair.

Shigata nudged the daybook open to its first page and said involuntarily, "Oh, shit."

"Why oh shit?" Hansen asked, and then looked over his shoulder. "Oh, shit," he agreed, and turned to Quinn, who hadn't been close enough to get a good look himself. "It's Margaret Ruskin."

Quinn, temporarily forgetting that he was working at moderating his language, swore somewhat more comprehensively. "What the hell is she doing here?" he then asked.

"She said she wouldn't be caught dead in a place like this," Hansen said, and involuntarily chuckled. "Guess she was wrong about that."

"Guess she was," Quinn agreed, without humor. Then he asked, "Who gets to call Jolene?"

"I'm afraid that's my job," Shigata said. "Anyway, we've got to get a formal identification."

A sedated—unconscious—alligator is an ungainly sight to say the least. The park veterinarian, beginning to dismantle his tranquilizer gun, looked up briefly as the larger alligator finally dropped its head onto its claws. "You've got about half an hour," he said, "and I recommend you work fast. When that big muthah wakes up he's gonna feel *mean*. First look at the alligators I've had since right after they got here," he added, "and I'm wondering has anybody told Hobby we're expecting babies?"

"What?" Shigata said.

The veterinarian pointed toward the grassy mound at the back of the pit. "That's a nest," he said. "In about another ten days there'll be about fifty baby alligators crawling down there. And Mama is going to be *very* protective."

"Shee-yit," Quinn said. "I'd rather be here now than then. But I'd really rather not need to be here at all."

"Might as well get it over with, before the medical examiner gets here," Hansen said, and vaulted over the wall again.

"Here," Shigata said, handing the camera to him. More distant photographs, of course, had already been taken, but some close-ups were going to be needed. "You take this," he said to Quinn, handing over a tape measure.

"What are you going to be doing?" Hansen asked.

"Watching," Shigata said. When Hansen, startled, looked back at him, Shigata said, "Rank Has Its Privileges."

Quinn shrugged and stuck the tape measure into his hip pocket, where it bulged startlingly. Too short to leap the wall as Hansen had done, he scrambled over it awkwardly and began to add measurements to the sketch he'd made.

"Look who's coming now," Jolene Robinson said. For a woman who'd been an elementary school teacher before becoming mayor, Shigata thought, she'd done a pretty good job of handling the sight of a dead and partially devoured city councilwoman whom she'd had to identify formally. But the fact remained that she was spending as much time as possible looking away from the alligator pit, which was why she was the first to notice the approach of Clifford Hobby.

Hobby, Shigata had thought the first time he'd seen him— and he had seen no reason to change his mind since—looked a little too smooth, a little too professional, a little too polished. Even now, summoned hurriedly to a body in a theme park on a hot morning in South Texas, he was wearing a gray silk business suit, a white French-cuffed shirt, a gray silk tie with little red rectangles on it. He didn't say anything as he approached; neither did Shigata.

Hobby walked directly toward the pit and stopped on the observation platform, where hurricane fencing replaced the rock walls that enclosed the other sides of the pit. He looked down. "This is a terrible, terrible tragedy," he intoned, and then turned. In a slightly more normal tone, he asked, "Does anybody know yet what happened?"

"Not yet," Shigata said, stepping onto the platform beside him. "Do you have any idea?"

"None whatever," Hobby said, and looked back into the

pit. "She opposed the building of the park, but of course you know that. I'm told that wasn't unusual for her."

"Hardly," the mayor said, brushing her red hair back from her forehead. "She'd opposed every suggestion for new business or industry of any kind for the last fifteen years at least, and probably longer. Fifteen years is all I know about."

"I'd heard that," Hobby said, mopping his face with a large white handkerchief. "Hot out here, isn't it?"

"No more so than usual this time of year," Shigata said.

Not replying to that, Hobby went on with his earlier train of thought. "But that wasn't her only objection to ArkPark. I'm told she considered it blasphemous. I can't imagine what would cause her to think that. Can you?"

Shigata, not trusting his voice at the moment, merely shrugged. Unlike Quinn, he didn't, in fact, consider it blasphemous; *ludicrous* was the word he would have been more likely to use. He was quite sure ArkPark would never reach its announced goal of possessing two—male and female—of every ritually unclean animal and seven of every clean one; the dioramas ranged from fairly realistic to garishly unrealistic; but it was with the rides that ArkPark had reached what Shigata considered the acme of tackiness. The parkgoer could ride through the air on either Elijah's flying chariot (two-passenger) or Ezekiel's flying chariot (six-passenger); be lowered with Saint Paul down the walls of Damascus; float around on Noah's Ark (complete with snack bar); drift down the Nile with baby Moses (avoiding mechanical crocodiles and hippos); ride a ski lift up Mount Nebo (which looked suspiciously like Disney's Matterhorn) to view the Promised Land (a particularly large diorama) with old Moses; or get caught in the fall of the walls of Jericho (every hour on the hour). Eventually, he'd been assured, he'd even be able to cross the Red Sea and swim in the collapsing walls of water.

Actually, he supposed, the whole thing might be rather amusing if he could manage to do as Hansen had done and put out of his mind its utter lack of dignity. But he wasn't able to make that mental separation. Neither, he suspected, had Margaret Ruskin been. Her opposition to ArkPark—loud, sustained, and voluble—had even included repeated environmental impact studies, although overall her opinion of environmental activism was scathing.

The city in general—overruling Ruskin—had welcomed ArkPark as a source of revenue, without stopping to think of its impact on city services, particularly the police department, in terms of traffic, crowd control, and emergency medical care. Already, less than two months after the opening of the park, some of the people who had disagreed with Ruskin were wishing privately, and in some cases publicly, that in this case they had listened to her.

"Do you think she could have just fallen in?" Hobby asked, still looking into the pit.

"Do you?" Shigata parried.

"I don't see how she could," Hobby answered. "You saw yourself, Sergeant Quinn had trouble getting in."

"Captain Quinn," Shigata corrected. "That's true, he did."

"We made the walls high enough that a child couldn't fall over and even an adult would have to work at getting over," Hobby said. "I don't see how she could have fallen in. Unless she was leaning in and was overcome by dizziness. And even then, I don't see how—if it happened during public hours—somebody wouldn't have seen her."

"Did she ever come here outside of public hours?" Shigata asked.

"If you'd asked me any time before this morning," Hobby replied somberly, "I'd have said she never came here at all."

"Hey, Shigata," Quinn called.

Shigata, abandoning his own dignity, said, "Excuse me," and clambered over the wall to join the other two, leaving the mayor with Hobby. "What've you got?" he asked.

Both Hansen and Quinn were squatting beside the head, which—surprisingly—had remained attached, if somewhat precariously, to the neck. "What do you make of this?" Quinn asked, gesturing to the left side.

Shigata looked closely, and then got up and walked over to the larger of the two alligators and lifted its upper jaw.

"I don't think that's a good idea," Quinn said, watching from where he continued to squat.

"It's asleep," Shigata said, looking carefully into the alligator's mouth. "Man, you've got bad breath," he told the beast, and closed its mouth again neatly. He returned to the head. "No thirty-eight-caliber teeth that I could see," he said. "And if Papa hasn't got them, it's a cinch Mama won't." But he paused long enough to check the other anyway.

Quinn stood up, opened the camera case, pointed the camera straight down, and took three photographs of the head, using three different lens settings. He reached for the head and then pulled his own head back, retching audibly. "I'm sorry," he said. "I can't. We need to see the other side of her head but I can't—"

"I don't blame you," Shigata said. "We've got to start carrying plastic gloves in every car." He reached for the head; Quinn's hand shot out to grab his.

"You've got a cut on your hand," Quinn said.

"A scrape," Shigata corrected. "That's all. I probably did it climbing over the wall."

"You don't handle a corpse without gloves if you've got a cut on your hand," Quinn said.

Hansen held his hands out in front of him, looked at each one, and then grasped the head and turned it to the right. It finished detaching itself from the spine, and Quinn jumped up, hands over his mouth, to run to the other side of the pit.

"He's got kind of a weak stomach, doesn't he?" Hansen commented, looking at the exit wound.

"That's okay, he picked a place where there isn't any evidence," Shigata replied. He stood up and approached Quinn. "Let me have the camera."

"I can do it," Quinn said.

"So can I," Shigata answered. "A lot more easily. Let me have the camera. You start looking for lead."

Quinn handed over the camera and looked down at the gravel. "You've got to be kidding," he said. "Anyway, how do you know one of them didn't eat it?"

"I don't know," Shigata said. "Jolene!"

The mayor leaned over the wall. "Yeah?"

"Would you see if you can get that vet back here?" he said. "He's got to figure out a way to get these alligators moved. And besides that he's got to X-ray them."

The mayor had returned to City Hall; the alligators continued to snooze in the shade of a huge mesquite tree the park builders had managed to spare; veterinarian Clay Lunsford, standing by with hypodermics in case one of the beasts began to wake up, continued to look uneasy. A large portable X-ray machine was on its way from the University of Texas Medical Branch in Galveston, although Lunsford had reported that everybody he'd talked to had laughed a lot when he'd explained what he wanted it for, and he'd finally had to talk to the head of the radiology department to get the machine dispatched.

One thing was certain: If the alligators *hadn't* swallowed the bullet, it was nowhere to be found. Donna Gentry from the Galveston Police Department identification section had already arrived, with a metal detector; she'd found all the water pipes that fed the alligator pit, and she'd found assorted coins and other debris that people had already tossed into the pit in the few days the park had been open, but she had not found anything even remotely resembling a bullet. Now she was packing the equipment in its carrying case.

"She wasn't shot here," Quinn said, looking down into the pit, his elbows resting on the rail. "The bullet went clean through, so it wasn't in flesh, so there wasn't any reason for one of them buggers to eat it. They're not like chickens; they don't swallow gravel."

Lunsford cleared his throat, and Quinn hastily added, "At least if they do, it's bigger than the gravel chickens swallow. I mean, how in the world would one of them buggers pick up a slug to eat it? He couldn't, unless it was in something bigger."

"I think you're right," Shigata agreed. "She wasn't shot here—but that makes it even weirder. How—and why—did somebody bring her in here and dump her in with the alligators, if she was already dead?"

"Maybe they wanted her not to be identified," Quinn suggested.

"That's a possibility for the short term," Shigata agreed. "But if we had an unidentified female corpse half-eaten by alligators and a missing city councilwoman, it wouldn't take too long to put two and two together. And whoever it was ought to have anticipated that."

"Maybe they figured there wouldn't be nothing left for us to know what happened," Quinn said. "I mean, if I'd been betting on it, I'd figure that big muthah down there"—he glanced at Lunsford, who'd used the phrase originally—"could swallow her in one gulp. And then who's going to know they swallowed a person?"

"In that case," Hansen said, "why did they put her purse down there?"

Shigata looked at him.

"The alligators might eat the woman," Hansen said. "They might eat her so thoroughly there really wouldn't be anything left. But they'd eat the clothes only because they were on the body, not because they wanted to eat the clothes. They wouldn't eat that bag. It doesn't smell like food, even to an alligator. It smells like chemicals. So if they didn't want her to be identified, it doesn't make sense they'd throw the bag in with her too."

"Hey, Hansen," Quinn said. "Maybe it was your friend Ralph Miner that did it."

"Oh, come on," Hansen said. "Miner wouldn't kill an ant."

"Maybe not," Quinn agreed, "but I wouldn't care to take bets on whether he'd kill a man who killed an ant. That fellow is plumb squirrelly."

"But why would he want to—"

"Because," Quinn said, "of that alligator purse and shoes she had. Maybe that's why he threw her in the alligator pit. To say that was what ought to happen to her for wearing shoes and using a purse made of alligator hide."

"That's crazy," Hansen said.

"Yeah, so's your friend Ralph Miner," Quinn said. "And speak of the devil—"

He had turned just in time to see Ralph Miner, video camera in hand, tranquilly lift the yellow police line tape from the sawhorses and posts it rested on and crawl under it. "Hey, Miner," Quinn yelled, "can you read?"

"Of course I can read," Miner answered. The gray-brown of his hair, which was rubber-banded into a loose ponytail, belied his youthful stride and expression, and he kept right on coming. Donna Gentry paused on her way to the Galveston ident car, the metal detector case in her hand, watching him.

"If you can read, then stay on the other side of the f— of the tape, like the tape tells you to," Quinn told him.

Miner continued toward the alligator pit, and Hansen said, "Ralph, back off, okay?"

Miner paused briefly and then continued toward the alligator pit. Shigata said sharply, "Stop where you are."

Miner did not stop, and Quinn headed toward him, grabbed him by the shoulder, and frog-marched him back to the line of evidence tape. "Under," Quinn said.

Miner did not go under the tape. He stood right where he had been, in the dappled sun and shade from the mesquite tree, when Quinn let go of him. As soon as Quinn stepped back a pace, Miner stepped forward a pace.

"That's called nonviolent resistance," Shigata said to Donna Gentry.

"Yeah, he's good at it," Gentry agreed, putting the metal detector kit down on the picnic table and continuing to observe.

Hansen, by now, was heading toward Quinn and Miner. "Ralph," he said tiredly, "I signed your bond once, but I can't do it twice. Now get on your own side of the police line, okay?"

"Not okay," Miner said.

"What do you think you're doing here anyway?" Hansen inquired. *"With* your video camera?"

"I paid my admission price to get in, same as anybody else," Miner said. "I'm legal. They haven't got an injunction barring me from the park yet."

"Not that you'd pay any attention to it if they did have one," Quinn said.

"Perhaps not," Miner agreed. "But the fact remains, I'm legal now."

Hansen began, "That doesn't answer—"

"I came to get pictures because I heard on the radio that some animals are being abused here—"

"What animals are those?" Quinn demanded. "And who's abusing them?"

"The alligators. You are. You've done something to the—"

"The alligators," Quinn said, "ate a city councilwoman."

"Yeah," Miner said, "Margaret Ruskin." His tone was dismissing. Apparently Miner considered it all right for the alligators to eat Margaret Ruskin, Shigata thought. "But that wasn't their fault," Miner added.

"Of course it was—"

"It was the fault of whoever gave her to them," Miner said rapidly. "Once the body was in the pit—"

"How did you know it was a body that got in the pit, and not a live woman?" Quinn asked, his curiosity somewhat exaggerated.

"It was on the radio," Miner said.

"Interesting," Quinn answered, "in view of the fact that we still aren't a hundred percent sure of that ourselves. I'll find out for sure if it was on the radio."

"It was," Miner repeated. "Anyway, whether or not she was dead when she went in the pit, the alligators acted on instinct. It wasn't their fault they ate her. And that doesn't give you the right to abuse—"

"Miner"— Shigata had moved quietly into earshot—"nobody is abusing alligators. They are anesthetized so that we can find out if they swallowed a bullet, and so that we could get the remains of the body and the other evidence out of the pit. But they are not being abused. They'll wake up just fine."

"Unless you decide to destroy them," Miner said.

"Unless we decide to destroy them," Shigata agreed. "But that's a decision that won't be made instantly, or lightly. In the meantime, the alligators are unharmed and will wake up just fine, quite soon."

"Just fine," Miner said bitterly. "And still caged."

"You caused enough trouble with the seals," Shigata said. "Don't start on the alligators now."

"I didn't start the trouble with the seals," Miner said. "The person who caused the trouble was the person who enslaved them. All I did was turn them loose."

"In the wrong ocean."

"It was the only ocean I could get to fast enough. It's cruel to keep seals caged."

"I will concede," Shigata said, "that it may be cruel to keep seals caged, even if they are—as these were—in a very large tank. However, in this case all appropriate permits were in order, and the seals were caged legally, which made it felony theft for you to release them, no matter what your feelings were on the matter—as you well know. Furthermore, it was equally cruel, if not more cruel, to release seals native to the northern Pacific into the Gulf of Mexico. It was particularly cruel to release *those* seals, because they had been raised in captivity and could not possibly survive without being fed."

"The Coast Guard brought them back," Miner said, with a sulkiness extremely unsuitable to his age and presumed dignity. "Anyway, I'm not talking about seals right now. I'm talking about alligators."

"I find it very difficult to believe," Shigata said, "that an animal with the IQ of an alligator cares in the slightest where it lives, as long as it has mud, water, vegetation, sunshine and shade, and enough food, and you've got to admit it's got all of those."

"It still shouldn't be caged," Miner said. "Animals aren't slaves. Anyway, why did that cop want to know what I heard on the radio?"

"In case you were lying," Quinn said.

"What difference would it make whether I was lying?" Miner asked. "I wasn't, but even if I was it's not illegal."

Patiently, Hansen said, "What Quinn is trying to say is,

he thinks maybe you're the one who killed Ruskin and gave her to the alligators."

"Why would I want to do that?" Miner asked, completely blankly. "I don't kill anybody or anything. I'm just here because of the—"

"Alligators," Shigata said. "We know. The alligators are not being abused. Look at it this way, Miner. If one of the alligators swallowed the bullet, don't you want us to get it out?"

"Only if you use noninvasive techniques," Miner said.

"Fine, we'll give the alligator a laxative," Shigata said, and Quinn hastily turned to hide his face. A snort of laughter burst from him anyway. "I mean, you don't want the alligator to get lead poisoning, do you?" Shigata added.

"You aren't going to hurt the alligators?"

"We are not going to hurt the alligators," Shigata said patiently.

"Maybe I'd better stay here and—"

"Maybe you'd better not stay here," Hansen said. "Ralph, I'm serious, nobody is going to do anything to the alligators, and I'm already having enough trouble convincing these guys you didn't kill Ruskin, so beat it, okay?"

"Your orders to him would be stronger," Shigata said sotto voce, "if you didn't keep saying 'okay' at the end."

"I know it," Hansen said, "but the problem is, I owe him."

Miner hesitated, watching the conference but not quite close enough to hear it. Then he turned and marched off, video camera dangling from his right shoulder. When he reached the tape, he turned back. "I'm going to get an injunction," he said, "forbidding you to destroy the alligators."

"Fine," Shigata said. "You do that."

"That man is more than just a little strange," Quinn said, watching Miner depart in unpressed cotton trousers and shirt, a belt made of a rope, and sandals homemade from recycled tires and rope. "He's the kind of strange that gives strange a bad name. An injunction protecting the alligators—!"

"More power to him," Shigata said wearily. "At least he's consistent."

"Consistent?" Quinn repeated.

"Consistent," Shigata said. "If he were wearing leather shoes and a leather belt and bitching about save the alligators when they aren't endangered anymore, I'd say he was hypocritical. Damn it, I don't want to kill the alligators anyway. But we might wind up having to."

"Why?" Quinn asked.

"To get the hands," Hansen said softly. "To get the hands."

"Steve," Donna Gentry said to Hansen, "why do you like that nut? I mean, I'm as much in favor of protecting the environment and animal life and so forth as anybody and probably more so than most people. I pay dues to Greenpeace and the Sierra Club and I recycle all my trash and compost all my garbage, and I think fur coats and alligator shoes are disgusting, but Miner doesn't think through anything he does. That thing with the seals"—she shook her head—"you'd think anybody'd have better sense than that. The poor things would have died out there in the Gulf."

Hansen, still staring after the departing activist, replied, "I don't like him much, now."

"But you said you signed his bond—"

"I did. I don't like him, in fact I'm not sure now I ever did like him, but I owe him."

"That's the second time you've said you owe him," Shigata pointed out. "Would you explain what you mean by that?"

"I was in college with him," Hansen said. "He was a couple of years ahead of me. See, another thing he doesn't approve of is cruelty to fourteen-year-old college freshmen."

"Fourteen-year-old college freshmen?" Gentry inquired.

"Yeah," Hansen said, glancing at her. "Me. Didn't you know my dad stuck me in college when I was fourteen?"

"No, I didn't. That sounds—"

"However it sounds, it doesn't sound half as bad as it was," Hansen said. "Sure I could do the work. That wasn't the point. The point was I was a freak. And nobody's very nice to a freak. Miner was a jerk even then, but he was a jerk that didn't approve of cruelty to anybody except police—he didn't regard police as human, of course, he was a typical sixties college student in that. But he protected me, the best anybody could." Hansen laughed bitterly. "It must have been quite a shock to him when I became a police officer. But as I said—I owe him."

Chapter 2

"So what do we know about her?" Shigata asked.

Once again Jolene Robinson was meeting with the police, this time in the small muster room outside the chief's office; as the mayor, she had had much more contact with the victim than the police had.

That was proving not to be a whole lot of use. Because Robinson answered, "Not much. She—I don't know, maybe she wasn't, but it seemed like she was always opposed to any new industry coming to town, or to spending money for improvements like sewers and storm drains and anything like that, and she was— Let me put it this way. She could get awfully sarcastic and even spiteful at city council meetings. But she kept track of her constituents, and she always got reelected. As far as her personal life—I know she was a widow, for what that's worth. And that's really all I know, or at least that I can think of right now."

"She owned some rent houses," Quinn said. "Nguyen and me lived in one right after I got back from Nam. My oldest boy, Johnny, he and his wife live in one of them now. I told him he was crazy to rent from her, but let's face it, there's not much in this town to rent, and he wanted to stay here. Danged if I know why."

"Why did you tell Johnny he was crazy to rent from her?" Shigata asked.

"Oh, Lord," Quinn said, and ran his hand over the lower part of his face. "She's—she was nosy. She meddled. She was bossy. She was unpredictable; you never knew whether she was going to like you or dislike you today and never mind how she felt about you yesterday. She'd rent but she wouldn't lease, so that there never was any agreement in writing, and then she'd interpret the oral agreement however she wanted to, including if she decided she wanted to rent to somebody else she'd evict a tenant on a few days' notice, which of course is illegal but what can you do about it? That enough for a start?"

"It's enough to tell me we better talk to all her tenants," Shigata said. "What kind of apartments were they?"

"Not apartments," Quinn said. "Houses. Well, three houses, one garage apartment. Small, all of them. The way they were laid out—" He started drawing a map on a piece of paper. "See, here's her house. And then there's this side street that runs down one side of her house, and you turn off this side street into this little court like, and there's three houses clustered there together all on this little court, and back of the little court, kind of at the back of her house and at the back of this house in the little court, there's this two-car garage with one car slot facing front, by front I mean toward her house, and one car slot facing back, and she uses the one that faces front, and the tenants in the garage apartment use the one that faces back. Like I said, small. All of them are two bedroom, one bath. Asbestos siding. Pretty ratty by now; I think they're about forty years old. The houses have carports, not garages."

"Pretty regular tenants?" Shigata asked. "Timewise, I mean?"

"They'd come and go," Quinn said. "Some would stay for years; others would be gone in a few months. Either she'd evict them for any reason or no reason, or she'd drive them so crazy they'd move out to escape."

"Maintenance?" Hansen asked.

"Oh, she maintained 'em well enough, considering she didn't know the first thing about maintenance," Quinn answered. "That wasn't the problem. The problem was she was just so damned *nosy*. When Nguyen and I lived there—course Johnny was about two then, and pretty soon Steve was on the way—times I thought she knew more about our business than we did. Back then we had a party line, and I think she was listening in half the time. That kind of thing."

"But she can't—couldn't—listen in on phone conversations now," Robinson objected. "So—"

"She'd still find a way to know," Quinn said. "That I guarantee you. Like she'd helpfully bring in your mail for you if you had overdue bills. Or she'd just happen to be out doing her yard work while you were having a quarrel."

"Blackmail?" Shigata asked.

"Nothing like that," Quinn said. "She just wanted to know because she wanted to know. Far as I know she never did anything with any of it, though I suppose if it was something illegal she'd report it."

Shigata made a note on an index card. "So it's at least a possibility that she was killed because she learned something somebody would have preferred she didn't know."

"Damn right it's a possibility," Quinn said. "Which doesn't mean we're going to find out what it was. There's no police department in the world with an intelligence network like the one she had."

"So who inherits?" Shigata asked. "That's always a possibility too."

Quinn shrugged. "She had two kids, a boy and a girl. They're grown up now, of course. I don't know where they live; I don't think they stayed around here. And no telling if they'd be interested in, uh, inheriting sooner than they would otherwise."

Shigata made another note on the index card. "We've got to find out. Obviously, finding them is number-one priority, because they've got to be notified. Who were her friends?"

Nobody said anything.

Shigata opened the alligator bag again, dumped its contents out on the muster room table, and reached for the daybook. Simultaneously Quinn reached for the plastic bag of ivory. Shigata paused. "That says something to you?"

"Not sure," Quinn said. "One thing, it's not hers, because she's had that real short hair for at least the last twenty-five years. She couldn't possibly wear these hairpins, and I don't think these pieces are twenty-five years old. My daughter-in-law, Mei Ling, Johnny's wife, she's got some ivory that looks a lot like this, but hers is a lot older. Hers is family stuff, used to belong to her grandmother. This looks like it could be something like a modern imitation of hers. A lot newer, anyway. This"—he shoved the bracelet over toward Hansen—"is almost white. Hers is real yellowed."

"It couldn't be hers?" Robinson asked. "Bleached with Clorox or something like that?"

"You don't bleach old ivory," Hansen said. "In the first place if you try you're crazy, because if the piece is any good to start with, it's more valuable if it's old, and in the second place it won't work anyway. Old ivory, no matter how well it's been cared for, has a lot of cracks and crazing. This stuff"—he shoved at it dismissingly—"this stuff is probably too new—" He stopped, looking at it. "Too new to have been imported legally," he said slowly.

"Not necessarily," Shigata answered. "Importation of ivory, even new ivory, is still legal provided the provenance is properly documented. There are some places in Africa and India where the elephant herds still get so big they have to be culled from time to time."

"Why don't they just move some of the elephants?" Robinson asked. "Find them another place to live?"

"Maybe there's not a place to move them to," Hansen said. "But you'd think there would be, wouldn't you? As long as elephants have been around, it'd be pretty crummy for 'em to go extinct in our lifetime. That's one thing I do agree with Ralph Miner on." Then, mentally, he shook himself. "But right now we're supposed to be finding out who made Margaret Ruskin extinct, and this isn't doing it."

"I'm not sure of that," Quinn said, poking at the jewelry again.

"What do you mean?" Hansen asked.

"Why did she have this stuff?" Quinn asked. "She couldn't have worn the hairpins, not as short as her hair was."

"You already said that," Hansen reminded him.

"So I'm saying it again. I don't see her wearing any of it; she was—she dressed sharp, but not exotic, and this stuff, this is exotic. So why did she have it in her purse?"

"There could be a dozen reasons," Hansen said.

"There could be," Shigata agreed. "But Al's right. Why did she have this in her purse at the particular time and place of her murder?"

"You got any ideas on how to find out?" Hansen challenged.

"Follow the rules," Shigata said, "and go through the normal procedures. That's how we find out most things. And you ought to know that." He opened the daybook and turned to the address section. "If the girl's married we'll play whaley finding her name," he said. "But the boy—"

Was easy enough to find. In the *R* section, a first name, Calvin, without a last name. An Amarillo telephone number and address, another telephone number with "office" written beside it. "Is that the son's name, Calvin?" Shigata asked, and Hansen nodded.

"Who'd name a kid Calvin?" Quinn demanded, and then answered his own question. "Never mind, I'm not the right one to ask, not considering my name. Who," he asked rhetorically, "would name a kid Albert? Okay. Who gets to call him?"

Shigata opened the book, took out that page, and headed for his office. He came back a couple of minutes later. "He says it'll take him until tomorrow to get here," he reported. "He's a lawyer, and he's got something this afternoon he can't reschedule no matter what. Says the girl is closer—Amy Conner. She lives in Livingston, and he told me she's usually home in the daytime. He gave me her phone number. So I called her, and she said she'll drive on down, ought to be here by about one thirty."

Jolene Robinson stared at him. "You called her on the telephone and told her her mother was eaten by alligators, and she's just going to drive right down from Livingston?"

"Well," Shigata said, "I told her her mother was found dead this morning."

"Right," Robinson said, "and what are you going to tell her when she gets here and what is going to happen if she turns her car radio on while she's driving down and hears about it that way?"

"You want to drive up to Livingston and get her?" Shigata asked.

"No, but—"

"There's not any right way to break this sort of news," Shigata said. "I told her it was murder, and I told her I'd explain when she got here. I asked if she wanted me to call her husband or clergyman, and she said she'd do it herself. What else was there to say at that point?"

"Probably nothing," the mayor admitted, "but it still feels tactless to me."

"I don't know what would be tactful," Shigata said. "I asked her about a consent search, and she said no problem. So I figure we'll wait—it's easier to do that than to get a search warrant. Al, you know the neighborhood, if you'd go talk to neighbors. Steve, go see about a court order to look at her bank records."

"You think we're gonna find anything there?" Hansen asked.

"No, but I think we'd better try anyway," Shigata replied. "It's a lot easier to do something that might be unnecessary than to try to explain in court why you didn't do it. But my guess is the real answer will be somewhere in city council records."

"Yea, verily," Hansen said. "Hand that book over, and let me get some information out of it."

He spent a few minutes copying information as Quinn got up and quietly left.

★   ★   ★

Finally alone in the office, Shigata rubbed tired eyes. The mayor had been right, he knew; he shouldn't have notified Amy Conner over the telephone, even with only a partial truth, especially because it was an extraordinarily gruesome murder and Margaret Ruskin was more or less a public figure. He should have called the police department in Livingston, or the sheriff's substation there, and had an officer sent out to break the news personally, so that there'd be somebody there in case of hysterics, in case of collapse.

So why hadn't he done that?

He didn't know why, except that he hadn't been a city police officer long enough yet to remember such things. He'd been an FBI agent for nineteen years, and that kind of problem isn't something the FBI normally deals with. An FBI agent, finally, takes orders. He makes a lot of decisions on his own, true, but he isn't, ultimately, the decision maker.

Now Mark Shigata was the chief of police, the decision maker; his—supposedly—was the desk where the buck stopped.

And he wondered, sometimes, like now, how good a job he was doing of it. Sometimes he suspected not very good; sometimes he suspected somebody else, like maybe Al Quinn, could have done better.

But it was too late to change his mind; he'd been only six months from his earliest possible retirement date from the Bureau when he quit to become the chief of an eighteen-officer police department, but there was no way he could get back into the Bureau now. And, to be perfectly honest with himself, there was no way he'd turn this police department—his police department—over to anybody else, not even Al Quinn.

Amy Ruskin Conner was, presumably, on her way. When she arrived he was going to be very, very busy, probably for the rest of the day. What he ought to do, if he had good sense, was go get some lunch.

Because he regarded himself most of the time as a man of moderately good sense, he stood up, walked out to the row of parking spaces in front of the police station, climbed into the Bronco with the city logo on it, and drove home.

And that might not be such a bad idea either, he reflected on the way. Because Melissa Shigata had grown up in Bayport, and for good or evil she knew where a lot of the bodies were buried in this town.

"I never met her," Melissa said, gravely—she did everything gravely—slicing ham.

When Shigata got a ham sandwich now it was turkey ham, guaranteed ninety-nine and ninety-nine one-hundredths percent fat free, and it was generally on either whole wheat bread or oat bran bread. Melissa made the sandwiches for him. She would not entertain the thought of his making his own sandwiches if she was at home. He supposed that her concern for his health, if it were less touching, would be either comical or infuriating, depending on his mood, but she had been abused literally all her life until she came to live in his house so many months before they were married, and obviously she felt she could not do enough for the first man ever who'd not hurt her. Shigata didn't know—feared he would never know—how to react to that. So he watched her slice the ham, spread the bread with Weight Watcher's cholesterol-free mayonnaise—not that he had a weight problem, but Melissa was concerned about cholesterol—and put a few pickles on the sandwich, but only a few because she was also concerned about his salt intake. She cut the sandwich into triangles and gave it to him on a plate, with a glass of milk.

"You're not eating?" he asked, as she sat down beside him.

She shook her head. "I already ate. I didn't know if you'd be home. But about Margaret Ruskin—as I said, I never met her. I heard stuff about her, of course, but everybody heard stuff about her. I don't know how much of it was true."

"You're not on the witness stand," Shigata said. "Hearsay might be useful. At least I'd know what some people thought of her, and what people thought of her might well lead me to whoever thought badly enough of her to kill her."

"Did you ever meet her alive?" she asked, then she laughed. That was still fairly new; it had been within the last six months that she had learned—or remembered—how to laugh. "That sounds silly, doesn't it? I mean did you ever meet her, of course. Did you ever see her alive?"

"A few times," Shigata admitted. "I think I'd have recognized her alive. But I sure didn't know her well enough to recognize her that way."

"I don't see how anybody could," Melissa said. "I can't help but wonder if Jolene recognized her, or if she just said she did because that was who she was expecting to see." Melissa did know the mayor, even if she hadn't known the councilwoman.

"I'm pretty sure she really recognized her," Shigata said.

"Anyhow," Melissa went on, "what I'm getting at is, you knew her well enough to know—well, she wasn't big, but she just had that air of authority about her. I—maybe I misled you a little, without meaning to. I said I never met her, and I didn't, but I saw her quite a few times. She—there were parties, you see, and he—" Melissa refused even now to mention the name of her first husband, whom Shigata and Quinn had shot and killed in his own driveway three years earlier. "He invited a lot of people," she went on, with an obvious effort, "and I—I had to meet them but I didn't really meet them, if you know what I mean. I mean I met her to say, 'Oh, it was nice of you to come, Mrs. Ruskin, won't you have a drink,' and that sort of thing, but I never really talked with her. But I always thought she'd have made a good police officer, or a good lawyer—she was always so good at finding things out, besides that air of authority she had. I don't know, I guess maybe when she was a kid it was just unheard of for a woman to go to law school."

"Not unheard of," Shigata said. "But certainly not as common as it is now. And if she had a pretty conventional upbringing—"

"Oh, she did," Melissa said earnestly. "That I do know. I heard her telling somebody that one night. I—I could have gotten to know her, if I'd wanted to, I guess. But she fright-

ened me. She really frightened me, the way she always found
things out—and there were so many things I didn't want
anybody to know. And I still don't. That's why I don't like
to meet people."

"Very few people have the intelligence network I'm told
she had," Shigata said gently.

"I know," Melissa said. "But if I went places—and I met
people who knew me before—"

Shigata put his hand over hers, picked her hand up, kissed
it. "I'd like to say what difference does it make," he said,
"but I don't think you'd want me to say that."

"No. I wouldn't. Because it wouldn't be true. "

The small hand-held radio that sat on the table while he
ate came alive suddenly. "Headquarters to Car One."

He swallowed his milk hastily and picked the radio up.
"Car One, go ahead."

"Chief, we got a female down here having hysterics saying
she's got to talk to you *now*."

Shigata glanced involuntarily at his watch. No, he was
right, it was clearly impossible for anybody to have driven
from Livingston this fast. Had she, for cryin' out loud, gotten
a helicopter?

Or was this some other female having hysterics, about
Margaret Ruskin, or about something else altogether?

"En route," he said and stood up.

"Take care," Melissa said without rising.

"I always do."

Her name was Moira DesJardines, a name Shigata had to
ask her to spell for him twice; she pronounced it "day-
zhardeen." She appeared to be about sixty-five. She was
wearing a black calico flounced skirt printed with multicol-
ored flowers and decorated with silver rickrack, a white puff-
sleeved, scoop-necked peasant blouse also trimmed with
silver rickrack, and black flats. Her hair was an extremely
improbable shade of red. She was *not*, she said with some
acerbity, hysterical. "I *merely*"—her tone italicized words—
"said that I *thought* that when my own dear sister was *mur*-

dered someone should have the *courtesy* to notify me *personally* and not leave me to learn it from the *radio*."

Shigata was inclined to agree that she wasn't hysterical; her eyes were quite dry, and her manner was more annoyance than grief or even shock. Just to set the record straight, he asked, "Whose sister are you?"

"Why, Margaret's, of course! Margaret Ruskin! How many murder victims do you have for me to be the sister of?"

"Only one, I'm thankful to say. But the reason we didn't notify you," he said, "is that we weren't—yet—aware that Mrs. Ruskin had a sister. Her children have been notified, of course, but I'm sure you can understand why they were undoubtedly too distraught to mention you to us. And the news was on the radio. My office hasn't released any information to the press yet."

"Oh, yes, it's on the radio and on the television." DesJardines fanned herself vigorously. "I'm sure dear *Amy* would have thought to call me *later,* but *Calvin* never has liked me, I'm *sure* I don't know *why*." Once again she fanned herself vigorously.

Shigata nodded toward Hansen, who was sitting at another table writing industriously and, apparently, making charts. "Is there any reason why you couldn't have talked with Sergeant Hansen instead of calling me back in from lunch?"

"I see *no* reason why I should be *fobbed off* with an *underling*," DesJardines said. "I should have the right to talk with the *man in charge*! It is not as if I were merely a *member* of the *public*; I am, after all, the victim's very own *sister*!"

"That's true," Shigata said, as gravely as he could. "How close were you and Mrs. Ruskin?"

"Oh, not *close* at *all*. She had her *own* life and I had *mine*; but still we were *sisters* from birth."

"I understand," Shigata said. "Well, maybe you could answer a few questions for us anyway. Had she seemed in any way different lately?"

"You mean *fey*, as if she *knew* something like this was going to *happen* to her?" DesJardines demanded.

"Nothing like that," Shigata said hastily. "More as if she had discovered something and didn't know what she was going to do about it."

"There was never a day in Margaret's life when she didn't know exactly what she was going to do with everything she knew and everything she had," DesJardines said, sounding for once halfway sensible. She glanced at Quinn, who had wandered in with his son Johnny, a Eurasian youth in his early twenties, tagging behind him, hands in his pockets just as Quinn's hands were in his pockets, posture identical to Quinn's. "Anyway, I hadn't seen her in several weeks."

"I want to show you something," Shigata said. He went into his office and returned with the plastic pouch of ivory. "We found this in Mrs. Ruskin's purse. Have you seen any of it before?"

"No," she said without hesitation. "That could not have been Margaret's. *Margaret* was an *anal retentive,* you see, and the person who wore *that* would be much more *open* in all matters."

"What?" Quinn said involuntarily.

Hansen looked up from his writing. "She says Margaret was uptight and a person who wore that jewelry would be laid-back."

DesJardines looked mildly astonished. "Well, yes," she said, "but more than that, a person who would feel, well, *comfortable* in that jewelry would be, well, *sensual* by nature, and Margaret definitely was *not.* Also, she would consider it in bad taste."

"Why's that?" Shigata asked.

DesJardines pursed her lips in thought before replying. "Dear Margaret, you see, was not at all *interested* in the *environment;* she felt all this concern for the *environment* was severely *overdone* and the situation was really not that *serious.* She was *wrong,* of course, but one simply could not *convince* her of that, but she said that so many people were concerned for the *environment* and *animal extinctions* and *that sort of thing* that to wear furs—not that one would wear furs in this climate, oh dear no—or ivory was in *very bad taste* and *politically unwise."*

Interesting, Shigata thought but did not say. "Let me get your address and telephone number," he said, "and I'm sure we'll want to talk with you more later. But for now, you—uh—need to get home and—uh—rest your grief in private."

Babbling not fully coherently about how considerate he was, *not* like that *awful* policeman who gave her the *ticket* last week in *Galveston,* Moira DesJardines allowed herself to be shepherded out of the building. Shigata, returning, grinned at Hansen and Quinn, and made the gesture of wiping sweat from his forehead and flipping it onto the floor.

"If dear, dear Margaret was an anal retentive," Hansen remarked, "dear, dear Moira is an anal expulsive."

"What?" Quinn demanded, very red in the face.

"Never mind," Hansen said. "Forget it." He resumed writing.

"Now that that's settled," Shigata said, reseating himself, "what's going on?"

"The judge is in a lunch meeting and won't be available to sign a warrant until after three," Hansen said, "but I've got the order for the bank records search made up so all he has to do is sign it."

"What are you doing now?"

Hansen looked at his notes. "I'm trying to deconstruct the case," he said.

"You're what?" Shigata said.

"It's a way of thinking of things," Hansen said. "I don't know if it's been applied to crimes before. But I thought it might be useful to give it a try."

"Explain."

"Well, you agree that a crime scene in a way is something that can be read?"

"I suppose so," Shigata said cautiously.

"Well, anything that can be read is a text, and if it's a text you can deconstruct it."

"Yeah, right," Quinn said. "So what are you gonna do, stick a piece of dynamite in it?"

Shigata, who had read a few comments in the *Wall Street*

Journal about the literary theory called deconstruction, said nothing. He just waited.

"You go at it several different ways," Hansen said. "You sort of find—well, it's—"

"It's what?" Quinn said. "Sounds to me as if you don't know what it is any more than I do."

"I do," Hansen said, "but I can't think of a good way to explain it to somebody that's not used to that kind of theory. Okay, it's like a dog food sack."

"Deconstruction is like a dog food sack?" Shigata said. "I don't think I've heard that description before."

"I'm serious," Hansen said with some dignity. "You know how, if you've got like a twenty-five-pound bag of dog food, it's fastened at the top with these strings, and if you pull on three of the string ends nothing happens, but if you pull on the fourth string the whole thing immediately comes unraveled? Deconstruction is like that. You try looking at it and sort of pulling at it from different angles, and when you find the right angle and you pull on it, then it all comes undone."

"So what does that accomplish?" Shigata asked.

"Then you can tell a lot of things about it, oh, like what things the person who created the text—which in this case would be the murderer—was so secure about, so to speak, that he didn't even have to write them. You find out what is there that maybe shouldn't be and what isn't there that maybe should be."

"So what's the difference between that and what we always do?" Quinn asked.

Hansen was silent for a minute. Then he said, "I can't think of a good way to explain."

"Then you don't understand it either," Quinn said roughly.

"I do. I just can't think of a good way to explain it."

"This discussion is going nowhere," Shigata said. "Steve, if you want to deconstruct this murder, do it on your own time. On city time, take care of city business. Al?"

Quinn gestured toward Johnny. "I brought him down here. Steve, I don't think you know my son Johnny, my oldest boy. Johnny, this here's Steve Hansen. I figured we all might as well hear at once, whatever there is to tell. Johnny, tell 'em what the situation is, in Mrs. Ruskin's rental units."

"What do you want to know?" Johnny asked.

"Whatever you can tell us," Shigata said. "I don't know anything about the situation; today's the first I knew she had any rental units. Of course, it's also the first I needed to know anything about her."

"Right," Johnny said. "You got some paper I could draw on?"

Hansen slid over a couple of sheets of the binder paper he was working on, and then moved closer himself, so that he could see what was going on.

Johnny drew a large right angle three-fourths of the way down the sheet, on the right-hand side, continuing the lines to the upper edge and the left edge. "This is the corner," he said. "Her house is on Crockett; that's the street that runs west to east." He drew a large square in the middle of the lower half of the enclosed square. "It doesn't always run west to east," he added, "but it does right here."

Shigata, by now wise in the ways of Bayport's not always comprehensible street system, nodded.

Johnny went on drawing. "Okay, this is Comanche; it runs north and south right here." He drew a second square, its lower-left corner almost touching the upper-right corner of the square he'd labeled "Ruskin." "This is where the Gonzaleses live. It's a garage apartment; Mrs. Ruskin uses one of the garage slots—has a breezeway that goes to it—and Pablo Gonzales, he uses the other."

"Who lives with him?" Shigata asked.

"Pablo and his wife, Joyce, and they've got a little girl, just a baby, let's see, what is her name? Tamara, that's it. She's just started to walk, and she's cute as a button. Pablo works for the railroad, and Joyce stays at home with the baby."

He drew a third square, its lower-left corner almost touching the upper-right corner of the garage apartment and its right side very nearly flush with the street he'd labeled "Comanche." "This is where Mei Ling and me live. I work at a gas station right now." He glanced quickly at Shigata; Johnny had applied for a job on the police department, and Shigata had not yet decided whether hiring him would constitute nepotism. "Mei Ling's going to school at College of the Mainland, until the baby gets here."

Shigata glanced at Quinn. "So you're going to be a grand-daddy?"

"Yep," Quinn said laconically.

"Congratulations."

Johnny went on drawing, another square, opposite the one marked "Gonzales." "This is where Lynette Evans lives. She's divorced and has three little girls. Jean, she's fourteen, and Mary, she's eleven, and Connie, she's nine. Jean baby-sits the Gonzaleses' baby when they go out, and Mary and Connie have both already applied to baby-sit ours."

"Where does Lynette work?" Shigata asked. The ivory jewelry, after all, did most likely belong to a woman.

"She's a secretary," Johnny said, "but danged if I know where she works. I'll find out, if you want."

"Not necessary now," Shigata said.

Johnny drew a fourth small square, to the left of the one he'd labeled "Quinn." "George Athanasopoulous," he said.

"What?" Shigata said.

Johnny spelled it. "He says nobody can pronounce it, and it's okay to call him George A., but I can pronounce it, and so I always do. He's a cook on an offshore drilling rig, works two weeks and then he's home a week. His wife's name is Irene, and she's a waitress at some truck stop café in Galveston, works nights a lot. They've got one boy, Junior, he's nineteen and he's got a job at ArkPark."

Shigata leaned forward. "And that's our first connection to ArkPark."

Johnny shook his head. "I don't think the guy that shovels out the elephant and hippo poop and shovels in the food is likely to be the one that fed Mrs. Ruskin to the alligators."

"Neither do I," Shigata said, "but he's still the first link to ArkPark, and we've got to look at him closely."

Johnny shrugged. "All I know about him is that he says if I know anybody that wants some elephant poop for like garden compost or anything like that he'll get it free and haul it for twenty bucks a pickup truckload."

"Tell him I want two truckloads," Hansen said instantly.

Shigata, who would have liked to have a truckload too but was afraid ordering it in the middle of a murder investigation would compromise his dignity, said nothing, as Johnny continued. "I'll tell him. But anyhow, Mrs. Ruskin, I don't know, I can't think why anybody would want to kill her. I mean, she's nosy and she makes people mad, but still—" He laughed uneasily. "Lynette was mad enough to kill her a couple of months ago, she said, but she didn't really mean it."

"What was she so mad about?" Shigata asked.

"Oh, she had to work late three days running and Jean was down with a bad cold and you can imagine what Mary and Connie got the house to looking like, and that was when the garage apartment was empty and the Athanasopoulouses were looking at it and Mrs. Ruskin said she hoped Mrs. Athanasopoulous was a good housekeeper and then she took Mrs. Athanasopoulous over to Lynette's house—this was during the day when the kids were in school and nobody was home—and Mrs. Ruskin just unlocked the door and marched in and showed Mrs. Athanasopoulous what the house looked like and said Lynette was a terrible housekeeper and if she'd known she wouldn't have rented to her, and she wouldn't have rented to her anyway except that the law made her. Did I mention Lynette's black? And, look, Lynette's not any worse a housekeeper than anybody else with no help and three kids and one of them sick, and that was just downright cruel."

"How did Lynette find out about it?" Shigata asked.

"Irene—Mrs. Athanasopoulous—told her, of course. She was mad too. Look, we're all minorities and we're all poor in that neighborhood. Mrs. Ruskin should have known if she didn't rent to poor people she wouldn't rent to anybody, not

the kind of places she's got. Had. And anyhow, after that the
Athanasopoulouses rented the place the Greenwoods moved
out of—they were Cherokee Indians—and the Gonzaleses
wound up renting the garage apartment. Not that it matters
who wound up where, but you might need to know."

Shigata decided he needed to give further thought to hiring
Johnny Quinn for the police department. But before he could
give further thought to that, or anything else, the dispatcher
stepped out of her cubicle. "Chief?" she said. "There's an
Amy Conner here to see you, and she's crying."

$\triangledown$

Chapter 3

THIS TIME IT REALLY was Amy Conner. The dispatcher, who also served as the desk officer, ushered her in.

She appeared to be in her early twenties. She had blue eyes and curly brown hair, and she looked about eight months pregnant. Her face was chalk white except for two spots of color on her cheeks, and she definitely was crying. "I didn't have the radio on driving down," she said to Shigata, her voice rising as she spoke, "because I thought they might be talking about—it—because of Mom being on the city council and all, and I didn't want to hear, but just before I got here I noticed my watch had stopped and I turned on the radio just long enough to hear what time it was, and they said—said— *What happened?* What really happened? They said *alligators*—is that—?"

"Call an ambulance," Shigata said to Quinn.

As Quinn headed for the dispatch room, Amy screamed, "I don't need an ambulance; I need to know what *happened!* Was it really *alligators*? Did somebody throw my mother to some alligators?"

"Your mother was shot," Shigata said quickly. "Yes, I'm sorry to say she was found in an alligator pit, but we are absolutely certain she was dead before she went into the pit. I realize even that's horrible, but it's not as if—"

35

Amy was sobbing wildly, and Shigata asked, "Where is your husband? I'll call him—"

"Right, you do that," she got out. "He's an army officer; he's in Saudi Arabia, one of those troops standing by in case Iraq does something else. You call my husband, and if we're real, real lucky he'll get here two days after the funeral and they'll let him stay two whole hours." Her sobbing was rising in volume.

Because the fire department was right next door to the police department, two emergency medical technicians arrived quickly. "What's going on?" one of them asked Shigata, as the other began to check the blood pressure of the now shrieking woman.

"She's Margaret Ruskin's daughter," he answered.

"Oh, shit," one of the technicians said. Into his radio, he began, "We got a white female, about eight months pregnant—" He strolled toward a corner of the room as he spoke, so much of the rest of what he said was inaudible. He raised his voice once, to ask over his shoulder, "What's that BP?"

"Two twenty over one thirty," the other said. "I say we ought to transport."

"That's what they say, too," the other said, sticking the radio back into his belt loop. "What's your name?" he asked Amy Conner. Turning to Shigata, he asked, "What's her name?"

"Conner. Amy Conner."

"Amy, can you hear me?"

She responded with something incoherent that might have been "Uh-huh."

"Amy, you've got to settle down for your baby's sake. Can you understand that?"

Another possible "Uh-huh."

"Okay, we're gonna take you to the hospital, just to be on the safe side. You understand?"

"Uh-huh." This time it was almost coherent.

"Damn," Shigata said, after the room was quiet again. "Damn, damn, damn, damn, that was my fault—Jolene was right, I should have had better sense—"

"It wasn't your fault," Quinn answered somberly, still staring at the door through which Amy had been carried. "Yes, you should have had better sense than to let her find out that way. But don't take all the blame. Save some of it for the son of a bitch that caused the problem. She'd have fallen apart like that whenever and wherever she heard about it. And you can't blame her for that."

"I don't," Shigata said.

"Or yourself," Quinn added. "When Nguyen was expecting Johnny, just before I managed to get her sent to the United States to stay with my mom where she'd be safe, her mom was hit by napalm. It was one of those friendly-fire accidents; they meant to be hitting a Vietcong village in the brush a mile or so away; but they got Nguyen's village instead and her mom was outdoors. Nguyen was inside, under a tin roof. By the time she got outside, the air strike was over and her mom was dead. You ever see anybody hit by napalm?"

"No," Shigata said. "I saw the picture, that little girl, the picture everybody saw. That was enough for me."

"About ten years old, stark naked, running and screaming? Yeah, everybody saw that picture," Quinn said. "The reality's worse. The pictures don't have the sound and the smell. Me, I'd rather be et by an alligator. What are we gonna do now?"

"You go get a search warrant for Ruskin's house," Shigata answered. "We've got to have a real good look and see if we can find out what she'd found out about whom. But before you do that, get vehicle registrations and find out about her car and get it on TCIC and NCIC; we've definitely got to locate it. Then get onto the search warrant. I'm going to go call her brother—Amy Conner's brother, I mean—again and see what he can tell me about the husband. If there's any way to get him home—"

"Get his full name, find out where he is, and then call the Red Cross," Quinn advised. "You're right; she needs him now a hell of a lot more than the army does. Okay. Car, then search warrant. Where's Hansen?"

"Headed for court," Shigata said. "His friend Miner's trial is supposed to start today, though I figure they'll reschedule it."

"I hope they'll reschedule it," Quinn answered. "We got enough on our plate, without Hansen being out of pocket because of those damned stolen seals—especially since Ark-Park got the seals back."

There was no problem with getting into the house; Margaret Ruskin's keys were missing from her bag (which suggested that something the killer wanted, and had had plenty of time to find, might have been inside her house), but a spare door key, along with a spare ignition key to the Pontiac they hadn't found yet, had been stuck inside a plastic pouch in her daybook. But getting keys, it turned out, had been a wasted effort. The house wasn't locked—and that, Shigata commented to Quinn, seemed a little strange.

The house looked comfortable. Well planned and built before home air conditioning, it would, Shigata thought, remain fairly cool even in the worst part of the summer. It was well shaded on the west and south, with deep-rooted trees that would weather any but the worst hurricanes; the windows were designed to catch the prevailing breeze, and the ceilings were high, as was appropriate in a place where cooling, not heating, was the problem ten months out of the year. Despite the hour, without lights it was dark inside the living room.

Shigata could hear Quinn, beside him, fumbling for a light switch. Then the lights came on, and Shigata involuntarily swore. "Shee-yit," Quinn agreed. Then he said, "You s'pose she always left it like this?"

"I wouldn't think so," Shigata answered. "Do you?"

Quinn took a comprehensive look at the damage. "No," he said. "Not likely."

Shigata took a couple of steps forward, into the chaos that probably had once been a neat living room. "Well, maybe we can get a fair idea of what size thing they were looking for by the kind of places they were looking."

"Either it was the size of a book or it was a piece of paper that could be folded and put in a book for safekeeping," Quinn said, looking at the floor. The walnut four-shelf bookcase that filled the space that in most houses would contain a television was empty, but it was evident the books had not been dumped out all at once by tipping the shelf. They were semistacked in several places on the floor, as if each had been pulled out of the bookcase, hastily examined, then put out of the way of the ongoing search.

Careful not to move anything, Shigata stepped through the living room into the kitchen. It, too, had been devastated, though not quite as thoroughly; evidently the searchers had not been hunting something likely to be found among the pans and canned goods. Either that or they had found what they were hunting before they got into the pots and pans and canned goods.

Quinn, following him, stepped into the breezeway that led from the kitchen into the garage. "Shigata," he said quietly.

Shigata, who had been looking at the debris on the counter, turned. "What is it?" He walked out into the breezeway.

"Have a look." Quinn stepped back to allow Shigata to see the dark blue Pontiac inside the garage. "How'd she get to ArkPark?"

"Somebody took her," Shigata said, "or else she drove herself and then somebody brought her car back here, when they came to search the house. Well, we've got our work cut out for us. You want to get the camera and fingerprint gear out of the Bronco?"

"Let's look at the rest of the house first."

It didn't take long to determine that the house had four bedrooms, three of which were full of books, and all the books had received the same treatment as the books in the living room. There were, it turned out, more books in the two-car garage, so many more books that the Pontiac had been parked, probably extremely cautiously—it was difficult to tell now, because all the books had been dragged out of the shelves—in the exact center of the space that was meant to hold two large cars.

*　*　*

"Is Ralph Miner in the courtroom?" the bailiff asked for the third time.

Ralph Miner still was not in the courtroom.

"Does the district attorney's office wish to present a motion to forfeit bail?" asked the judge.

Steve Hansen stood abruptly. "Your Honor," he said, "I posted bond for the defendant, and I'll find him."

"See to it that you do, Sergeant Hansen," the judge said. To the bailiff he added, "Call the next case."

Hansen left the courtroom.

"—Don't know," Hansen, standing just inside the garage door, one foot resting absently on a stack of books, which, like all the rest of the books, were far too dusty to hold fingerprints, was saying, "but I don't like it." He glanced down. "I thought I had a lot of books, but I've never seen anything like this in my life. Anyhow, about Ralph, if I hadn't seen him this morning, I'd be wondering if he'd skipped. But—"

"But we did see him this morning," Quinn said. He was farther inside the garage, sitting on a stack of *Encyclopædia Britannicas* between Hansen and Shigata, who was sprawled across the front seat of the Pontiac. "At a murder. I was halfway kidding when I said then he could have done it, but now—"

"If he did it," Hansen said, "then what the hell was he doing there this morning? You know as well as I do that old saying about the killer always returning to the scene of the crime is crap."

"It's also crap to say the killer never returns to the scene of the crime," Shigata answered, continuing to dust for fingerprints because he was a lot better at that task than Quinn was, and Hansen hadn't been there when the job started.

He laid wide pressure-wound tape over a print, pressed it down carefully with his fingers, lifted it again, and pressed it down carefully on the edge of a glazed white card; then he cut it close to the roll with his pocketknife. He very carefully labeled the location—front of rearview mirror, the year of the

Pontiac, the tag number—then added the case number, date, and time, initialed it, and handed it to Quinn. Quinn initialed it also and added it to the growing stack of cards in his shirt pocket.

Then Hansen said, "I still can't see Ralph killing anybody or anything. He'll walk around an ant on the sidewalk rather than step on it. I think if he ever got lice he'd stop washing his hair, to avoid inconveniencing them."

Quinn chuckled, deep in his throat. "That's drastic," he said. "But I still say it doesn't prove anything about what he would or wouldn't do about a human being who was wearing alligator hide—or killing ants."

"To the best of my knowledge he's never owned a gun," Hansen added, "and I can't see him learning how to use one."

"Looks like she was shot at contact range," Quinn said, "and how much aiming does that take?"

"You still have to know how to load the gun," Hansen argued, "and you still have to be—gun conscious. What I'm saying—part of what I'm saying—is I don't think Ralph would *think* to use a gun, even if he did decide to kill somebody. Guns just aren't a part of his mental universe. Throwing somebody to the alligators—maybe. I'd believe that a lot sooner than I'd believe he'd use a gun, in any situation or under any provocation whatever."

"Be that as it may," Shigata said, maneuvering himself out of the front seat, "you've still got to go find him, before he really does forfeit bond and you find yourself living on the street. I told you putting up your house to bond him out—"

"Was stupid," Hansen said, moving away from the door so that Quinn and Shigata could get past him into the breezeway. "Okay, it was stupid. I still did it. And now I've got to go look for him. Okay. Unless I find him sooner, I'll be on that the rest of the day. And probably Friday too. I could strangle the son of a bitch," he added over his shoulder, heading for the house door. "Do a favor for somebody and what do you get? Shafted!" The door opened. A moment later it slammed behind him. It was followed shortly by the slam of the front door.

"There's not much left of the day," Quinn commented, strolling into the living room and looking at his watch. "It's four fifteen now. What are we gonna do about this mess?"

"We didn't make it."

"I know we didn't make it," Quinn said. "But when that woman, Amy Ruskin everwhat her name is now—I still think of her as a little kid on a tricycle—gets out of the hospital, she's going to come here. And is that what we really want her to see?"

"It's not our responsibility," Shigata said, "but I see what you mean. Well, let's finish searching, and then—"

"I don't know what else we're looking for," Quinn said.

"I don't either," Shigata agreed. "I'm just hoping whatever it is, we'll recognize it when we find it."

Quinn let his gaze slide comprehensively around the kitchen, dining room, living room. "Chief," he said, "most likely either it never was here to start with or they already got it."

"That's probably true. But we've got to look anyway."

In the end, it was Randy Quinn, eleven, who found it. Shigata and Quinn had given up on the search about seven thirty, and Melissa and Nguyen, along with Shigata's daughter, Gail, and assorted Quinn offspring, had come to help make the house presentable again before Amy Conner saw it. Randy threaded his way carefully around books to emerge from what seemed to have been designed as a guest bedroom, approached Quinn, and said, "Dad, I think I goofed."

"How did you goof?" Quinn asked, returning music books to the inside of the piano bench.

"I tried to use the bathroom in there and it won't flush."

"The bathroom in where?" Quinn stood up. "I guess you better show me."

Moments later, Quinn shouted, "Chief, I think you better see this."

Shigata paused on the way; he'd just heard a television cut on. He looked into the main bedroom—what had been Margaret Ruskin's own room—to see Todd Hansen, now seventeen, sprawled on the bed. "Todd," he said, "what are you doing?"

"Watching TV."

"Uh-huh," Shigata said. "Why here? Couldn't you just as well be doing it at home?"

"Ed Quinn brought me over here," Todd pointed out, sounding slightly aggrieved.

"Ed Quinn is picking up books," Shigata said. "Why aren't you?"

"I didn't put 'em down."

"Todd," Shigata said, "get to work, or hit the road, one or the other. Now turn off the television."

Todd stood up, slouched over to the television, and turned it off. "How'm I supposed to get home?"

"You've got feet," Shigata said. "Use 'em."

"It's two miles."

"So what? You're healthy."

"But—"

"I'll say it once more," Shigata said. "Get your ass in gear, or get it out of here."

Without replying, Todd slouched into the living room and resumed picking up books.

She must have known somebody would be looking for it, and she must have guessed this was a place nobody would think of looking. Apparently she would have been right, if Randy hadn't tried to flush. Not that it was an unusual place for things to be hidden, Shigata thought; he hadn't looked there because he didn't figure Ruskin, who was certainly not a part of the drug culture, would think of the toilet tank. And the fact that whoever killed her hadn't thought to look there was also interesting; it suggested a murderer or team of murderers with no drug involvement.

She hadn't done a bad job of it, all things considered, Shigata thought. Many people put bricks or jars in a toilet tank, so the toilet will use a little less water. Nobody would have noticed until the next time the tank was opened, if the jar had been full of water so that it would have stayed put.

But because it was full of ivory and air, it floated, and that interfered with the flush mechanism.

Shigata had the pickle jar on the kitchen table now, open, the ivory—new and white, like the ivory from the bag in the purse—out on a paper towel. Another bracelet, another set of hairpins, carved just like the ones that had been in her purse. And a necklace made of little carved elephants interspersed with ridged ivory beads. He was dusting them for fingerprints, very carefully, using mag powder, in case whoever she had gotten them from had left his or her fingerprints on them. But nothing was coming up.

But if that—the ivory—was what they were after, if she had somehow taken it away from somebody, so that was what they wanted back—then why did they, whoever they were, throw the purse into the alligator pit with the other jewelry still in it? Or did somebody toss the purse in after her without even looking in it? But if that was the case, how did they get her keys? Because presumably they had gotten the keys out of the purse.

Of course, they may not have had the keys to start with, Shigata reminded himself, examining the ivory carefully with a magnifying glass in the hope of seeing print traces he might have missed using only his eyes. She might not have driven her car to ArkPark; she could have gotten there some other way. Somebody might have taken her; she might have taken a taxi. She might even, as unlikely as that seemed, not have locked the door to her house before she left.

But if that were the case, Shigata and Quinn should have found her keys in the house or the car, and they hadn't.

Maybe she *lost* the keys somewhere, Shigata thought. In that case, the keys in her daybook could have been the only ones she had, until she had a new set made. That idea carried the assumption that whoever had entered the house had done so without keys, even if the house was locked, but that certainly was not impossible no matter how good the locks were. They'd seen no sign of forced entry, but forced entry doesn't always leave signs.

"Oh, hell," Shigata said and gathered the ivory into plastic bags. "I'm going up to the hospital and see if I can get in to see Mrs. Conner."

Amy Conner was lying on her right side, her left knee drawn up, the top of her head toward the wall, facing the door. In the semidarkness, her blue eyes looked enormous.

"May I come in?" Shigata asked from the door.

"Uh-huh," she said without moving. "You can turn on the overhead light. The switch is right by the door."

After turning on the light, Shigata stepped on into the room, found a chair, and lifted it around to the bedside. He sat down. "I don't know if you remember me, Mrs. Conner," he began.

"I remember you," she said. "Chief Shigata. You called me at home. And please call me Amy. When somebody says Mrs. Conner, I always look around to see if my mother-in-law is following me. She's a very sweet mother-in-law, actually, but I'm not her."

"Amy, I owe you an apology."

"What for?" Her voice was a little drowsy, but she would be only lightly sedated, Shigata thought. The doctors wouldn't dare give her heavy sedatives now; doing so would sedate the baby too, and an unborn baby is too sensitive to that kind of medication.

"I shouldn't have let you find out from the radio," he said.

"It wasn't your fault." Carefully keeping herself covered by the sheet, she sat up. "The newspeople are going to say what they're going to say. My mom told me that years ago."

"But I know that too. So I should have called the police department where you live and had somebody notify you face-to-face."

She shrugged. "It wouldn't have made any difference. I'm sorry I fell apart." Then, before he had time to answer that, she said, "On the phone, you said something about needing my signature. I can sign whatever it is now."

"It's not necessary. It was a consent to search form, so that we could check your mother's house for evidence. But we went on and got a search warrant."

"Did you find anything?" She sounded a little more alert; she regarded him evenly.

"We found something. But we don't know how relevant it is, and we don't know if it was all there was to find."

"Oh?"

"Somebody else searched the house, before we got there," he explained.

"The—the person who did it? Who killed my mother?" There was renewed strain in her voice. "Because I was going to go stay there, at the house, after I got out of the hospital, but maybe I better not—"

"You'd better not," Shigata agreed. "In fact, I'd rather you didn't even go over there without one of my officers with you, just to be on the safe side."

"How could you tell somebody else had been there? Did they make a pretty big mess?"

"They did, yes. They dragged out all the books."

"*All* the books?" she repeated unbelievingly. "It'll take me a hundred years to pick that up!"

"You won't have to," Shigata said. "We—Quinn and I, and our wives and kids—cleaned it up for you."

It was the first time he'd seen her smile. "That was nice of you." The smile faded. "What did you find?"

He pulled the bed table into place and laid the bags of ivory on it. "This was in her purse, which was found with her," he said, "and these were hidden in the house. Have you seen any of it before?"

She looked at the jewelry without touching it. "No," she said. "Is that real ivory, or plastic?"

"Almost certainly real ivory," Shigata said. "I looked at it through a magnifying glass. I'm no expert on ivory, of course, but I don't think plastic would look like that."

Amy shook her head. "My mother wouldn't have had that. She thought things like that were in very bad taste. She said it was pretty but too many people disapproved, and people— especially if they were in politics, but really everybody— should have a decent regard for other people's opinions, unless they were harmful."

"Your mother sounds like a pretty intelligent woman," Shigata said. "Do you know why she opposed building Ark-Park?"

Amy nodded. "She said the Reverend—so called—Clifford Hobby was a fake, and sooner or later he'd bail out and the city would get stuck holding the bag. And she said it would cost the city a lot more in services than it would produce in revenue."

"She was right about the cost," Shigata said ruefully. "As to Hobby—well, he hasn't bailed out yet."

"Give him time," Amy said.

"When was the last time you talked to your mother?"

"Yesterday," Amy said. "She called me about three o'clock."

"What did you talk about?"

"The baby. That was all. She didn't tell me she was up to anything. But—she didn't usually call me. So I wonder now if she had some sort of a hunch that—that something might go wrong."

"Did she ever try to investigate things on her own?" Shigata asked as delicately as possible.

"You have undoubtedly been told," Amy said, "that my mother was probably the nosiest woman God ever put on this earth. It was perfectly true. She couldn't stand not knowing anything."

"Was that the reason for all the books?"

Amy smiled slightly. "That was the reason for all the books," she agreed. "And she watched people all the time. Everybody. So—would she investigate something? Sure she would. But what was she investigating this time? I don't know, Chief Shigata. She didn't tell me. She probably didn't tell anybody. She usually didn't, not until she'd found out what she wanted to know."

"The pictures I've got of her seem to vary pretty widely," Shigata told his wife, over carry-out hamburgers. "From what Amy Conner tells me, she sounds pretty practical, pretty reasonable. But the Quinn boy's story—and especially about Mrs. Evans—"

"Mark," Melissa said, "people can be practical and prejudiced both. And reasonable and spiteful both." She dipped the end of a french fry into a small bowl of catsup and nibbled on it.

"You're not to repeat any of this at school," Shigata said to Gail.

"I never do— Can I go to ArkPark tomorrow?"

"Certainly not," Shigata said, "it's Friday."

"It's a teacher workday, not a school day," she argued, "and Mom said I could go if it was all right with you."

"Then it depends on who you're going with. You certainly can't go alone."

"Me," she said, "and Ed Quinn, and some of his brothers and sisters, and some of his cousins, the Hoa kids, and of course *Todd*"—she made a face—"because we can't leave *him* out even if everybody wants to. But Ed said he'd be in charge."

Ed Quinn was eighteen and, like all the Quinn children, completely dependable. "In that case, you may go," Shigata said. "Do you need some money?"

"I saved my allowance," she said with dignity. "But— uh—"

"I'll give you some money," Melissa said. She had desisted in her attempt to give away all of her former husband's money when it dawned on her that Gail might at some point in the future have a use for some of it.

"This is stupid," Todd Hansen said, kicking at his hackeysack.

Gail Shigata, climbing rather dizzily off the roller coaster (disguised as a series of Roman galleys) and shaking the seawater off her face and hands (this ride had billed itself as "Get Shipwrecked with Saint Paul," and the water, at least, had been real), was inclined to agree. Janie Quinn, also fifteen, probably would have agreed, but she'd started throwing up when Elijah's Chariot rose a little precipitately, and had just returned, with Angele Hoa, from the first-aid station.

"Let's go look at the aquarium," she proposed now. "That shouldn't make even me sick."

"Who wants to look at a bunch of stupid fish?" Todd demanded.

"It was still closed twenty minutes ago," Don Quinn said, ignoring Todd completely.

"It was s'posed to open at nine thirty," François Hoa said, "and it's nine twenty-five now."

"What makes you think it'll open on time?" Todd asked. "Nothing else has around here."

"Maybe it will," François said. "We might as well go find out. You probably don't know, but Janie wants to be a marine biologist, and she's not going to give any of us any peace until we go look at her fishy-fishies. And none of us are allowed to go off on our own. You know what Dad and Uncle Al said."

"I'll go off on my own if I want to," Todd muttered.

"That's what you think," Ed Quinn said tranquilly.

"Who's gonna stop me?"

"Me," Ed answered, "and don't think I can't. Or won't."

Todd Hansen loomed a full head above the tallest of the Quinn and Hoa kids, and Ed wasn't the tallest. But looking at Ed's face, Todd shrugged. "I guess I'll stick around."

"I guess you will," Ed agreed, "and we'll all trot over to the aquarium together."

"You can always leave me there," Janie pointed out, "so nobody else has to be bored with the fish, and you can come back and get me later. That's not going off on my own."

"It's the same thing," Ed said.

"Not if Angele stays with me."

"What makes you think Angele *wants* to stay with you?"

"I'll stay," Angele said. "I want to think, and I think just as well with fishes as without them."

"There," Janie said triumphantly. "And see, it is opening. Right on time, too."

It did not, of course, call itself an aquarium; it contained an underwater diorama of Pharaoh's army drowning in the Red Sea. But the newspaper had been ecstatic over the salt-water aquarium and the variety of fish, crustaceans, and anemones, and Janie had been counting the days until she got a look at them.

She pushed open the now unlocked door and entered the dank quietness, followed by her cousins and friends.

The charioteers (wax) were one-fourth life size. The spears and chariot wheels (wood, weighted with lead) strewed the bottom of the huge glass tank, and the fish swam heedlessly among them—and between the full-size legs of the long-haired man in cotton pants and rubber and rope sandals, and the metal legs of the tripod of his video camera.

Janie screamed and covered her mouth; then there was no sound at all for a moment.

Into the silence, Todd Hansen said, "I know him! That's Ralph Miner! He's a friend of my dad." Then he added, "The newspaper said there were sharks in that tank. It looks like there aren't any after all. Too bad—if there were, then we'd *really* see something."

Ed Quinn turned thoughtfully and punched Todd in the mouth before saying, "Don, go find a phone and call Dad."

▽

Chapter 4

ONCE AGAIN PART OF ArkPark was surrounded by yellow evidence tape. Inside the evidence tape were witnesses; four of the Quinn kids (Janie had temporarily departed), four of the Hoa kids (Angele had temporarily departed), Gail Shigata, and Todd Hansen.

"So why did you slug Todd?" Quinn asked, as he stood on the ground beside a stone wall outside the diorama and waited for volunteer divers—the city had used them before; this near the coast there was frequent need for divers—to retrieve the body of Ralph Miner.

"It felt like a good idea," Ed replied. He also was standing, a little distance downhill, with his hands on the shoulders of five-year-old Debbie Hoa, the youngest of the party that had gone to ArkPark.

Todd, sitting on a brick wall under a mesquite tree nursing a fat lip, tried to glower and succeeded only in looking sullen. Gail, sitting on the same wall, had pointedly positioned herself about six feet away from him, beside nine-year-old Teresa Hoa and thirteen-year-old Don Quinn and François Hoa. Joe and Randy Quinn and Jacques Hoa, all eleven, were sitting on the ground under another tree, having a discussion of their own.

"Don't you think it might be a good idea to apologize?" Quinn asked.

"No," Ed said. "He had it coming, for being a horse's rear end. You feeling better, Debbie?"

"Uh-huh. Why was that man's face purple?"

"I don't know," Ed answered.

"Why was his tongue sticking out?"

"Because his face was purple."

Debbie giggled. "You're silly. Can I go find Angele?"

"Angele and Janie went to find us all some Cokes," Ed said. "And I don't know where they went. So we better stay here and wait for them. Why don't you go sit with Gail, and let me go talk with my dad for a minute?"

"Okay."

Debbie scampered away, and Ed walked up the hill toward the top of the large seawater tank, with Quinn following him. On the east was a seating area where people could congregate to watch the seals; the ground sloped down toward the west, so that people could enter the building and look through thick glass at the diorama and the seal tank, which—to protect the rare fish in the diorama from voracious seals—were separated by a sturdy steel mesh. "He was strangled, wasn't he?" Ed asked. "Not drowned?"

Quinn nodded. "That's what it looks like. You saw the strap around his neck?"

"Yeah. I think it was part of what he was using to carry the video camera with. Dad, about Todd. I'm sorry," Ed said softly, glancing back down at the kids sitting on the wall. "I know we're all supposed to be nice to Todd, to help him get over things. Well, I've been nice as long as I can. I punched him because he needed somebody to punch him, and I'll do it again if I need to. You know who he reminds me of?"

"No, who?"

"Remember when I was a little kid and you read me all those Narnia books?"

Quinn winced. "Don't let anybody hear you say that; you'll ruin my tough-guy image."

"He reminds me of Eustace Scrubb or whatever his name

was. The kid that turned into a dragon. Too bad there's not some way to turn Todd into a dragon for a while. Dad, I had to punch him, and I'd do it again. We're not going to teach him manners by letting him get away with having none."

"You're probably right," Quinn said. "But I hope you can understand my point of view.

"I do," Ed answered. "He's damn fool enough to charge me with assault, if he can get his dad to let him, which I don't think he can, but if he can, well, that's the breaks."

"Okay," Quinn said. "As long as you know what you're doing." He glanced down at the tank. "I'd like to know how much Hobby spent on this place to start with, and how much it costs to run. I've seen city zoos—big cities, at that— a lot less elaborate. If it's a scam, it must pay damn well."

"If you knew what the scam was, you might know why this guy is dead," Ed remarked.

"This guy and Margaret Ruskin too," Quinn agreed. "I don't know, maybe it is on the level. Maybe I've just been a cop too long to see the whole picture."

"And maybe this guy was strangled by a pissed-off sea lion," Ed returned. "But somehow I don't think so."

"But if it was somebody at—or involved with—ArkPark that did the murders," Quinn said, "why leave the bodies here? That just draws attention to ArkPark. Ruskin could have been put anywhere after she was shot; nobody had to throw her to the alligators. And maybe they thought the alligators would eat her completely and nobody would know, but nobody thought the fish were going to eat Ralph Miner. So nobody was trying to hide him—they were trying to make sure he was very much noticed, which says that's probably the case with Ruskin too. And if anybody was doing something here, it doesn't make sense they'd want us to look close at ArkPark."

"Ever hear of 'The Purloined Letter'?" Ed asked, watching Janie and Angele crawl under the yellow tape, past the patrolman stationed by it to keep intruders out, to begin to distribute paper cups of Coke.

"What does that have to do with anything?"

Ed shrugged. "If the best way to hide something is in plain sight, maybe the best way to draw attention away from something is to draw attention to it. Or maybe they figure it's something the police wouldn't notice because police don't have the kind of nosy minds that Ruskin and Miner had. When's Chief Shigata going to get here? And Sergeant Hansen?"

"Soon, I hope."

One of the divers came up out of the tank, propelling the limp body, and both Quinns went to help lift it out of the water. Seen closely, the purple-suffused face with its bulging eyes and protruding tongue, with the foam still visible around the mouth despite its long submersion, was more horrible, more grotesque than it had looked in the water. The first diver clambered out, to look down at the body at his feet. "Somebody didn't like that dude one damn bit," he said, "and that's a fact."

The other diver went back down for the video camera. Handing it up to Quinn, he said, "I'm going to see if there's anything else down there."

Quinn turned, to see Hansen approaching. Hansen ducked under the yellow tape, strode on into the secure area, and then paused under the mesquite tree. "What happened to you?" he asked Todd.

"Ed Quinn punched me."

"Why'd he do that?"

"I don't know."

Gail, without moving from where she was sitting, said very loudly and clearly, "Because he said he wished there'd been a shark in the water with Mr. Miner."

"Then I'd say you had it coming," Hansen said. He walked on up the hill, to look at Ralph Miner's body. "Damn it," he said. "Damn it all to hell and gone anyway. He was a harmless eccentric, why'd anybody want to kill him?"

"My guess is he wasn't that harmless," Quinn said. "At least somebody figured he wasn't." He went silent then, realizing suddenly that Hansen was crying. "Steve?"

"I'm all right," Hansen said, not sounding totally all right.

"It's just—okay. Environmentalism. It comes in a lot of forms, good and bad, smart and stupid. You see people risking their own necks, out in small boats in the middle of Japanese whaling fleets, and you see people risking other people's necks, doing jackass things like putting metal and explosive charges in big trees loggers are going to chop down. Miner—he was eccentric, he always was, even when he was a kid, and the older he got the more eccentric he got. He did dumb things, sometimes, like trying to free those damned seals. He made a lot of noise and got people to look at him and laugh at him and maybe, just maybe, once in a while, to think about what he was saying. But I'd have said he didn't really risk anybody's neck, his or anybody else's."

"Happens you were wrong," Quinn said.

"It looks that way. Well. Damn. So what do we do now?"

"Back off five yards and punt," Quinn suggested.

"What have you been doing?" asked Shigata, who had silently joined them.

"Me?" Hansen said. "Since yesterday afternoon, hunting him." He nodded toward the body.

"How far had you gotten?"

"I can tell you where he was every minute up until three fifteen yesterday. For all the good that does."

"Then stay with it," Shigata said. "Find out where he was at four fifteen, and five fifteen, and keep going until you lose the trail—and maybe it'll be interesting to see just exactly where you do lose the trail."

"Now?" Hansen said.

"Might as well. If you're up to it." Shigata, too, had seen the traces of tears on Hansen's face.

Hansen shrugged. "I'm as up to it as I'm going to be. Okay." He went back down the hill, passed Todd without saying a word, and kept on going.

"And that's part of the reason Todd is such a jackass," Ed said softly.

"What is?" asked Shigata.

"That. His dad ignores him, or talks at him, or sometimes talks to him, but he never does talk with him. And right now

I figure that kid needs to talk with somebody."

"Maybe his dad doesn't know how," Shigata suggested. "My dad didn't. And I came out all right."

"If he doesn't know he could learn," Ed retorted. "Somebody's got to reach that boy soon or he's gone. Maybe your dad didn't talk with you, but I'll bet somebody did." Then he chuckled wryly. "All right, so I'm only a year or so older than he is and I'm talking like Methuselah. But I've got good sense."

"Some of the time," Quinn suggested.

"Some of the time," Ed agreed. "And I'm not a hundred percent sure Hansen, with all his book smarts, has any people smarts—at least where his son is concerned. Would I be reading it right if I were to guess you'd like me to get out of the way so you guys can work?"

"After I ask a couple of questions," Shigata said.

"So ask."

Shigata glanced at the body. "Never mind," he said, "I'll ask them later. I figure if you knew anything that might be useful you'd volunteer it."

"That I would. All I can tell you is, we were taking Janie to see her fishy-fishies, as François puts it to rib her, and that's what we saw instead of, well, besides the fish. And then Todd made his wisecrack about wishing there'd been a shark in there and I punched him and then I sent Don to call Dad and then I got the others out of the building and sent Angele and Janie to get everybody Cokes and I stayed by the door—there's only one—to make sure nobody else went in."

"Okay," Shigata said. "I'll get a formal statement from you later. Right now I don't think we'll need to bother the other kids, but you can tell me later on who they all are, can't you?"

"Oh, sure," Ed said. "That's all?"

"For now, yes," Shigata said. But then he said, "Wait a minute. What, exactly, was Todd's wisecrack about the shark?"

"Oh, I don't remember exactly," Ed said. "Something like, the newspapers said there was a shark in the tank and he wished there really was because then we'd really see something."

"Anything else?"

"Not that I can think of."

"Okay," Shigata said. "Thanks."

Ed went down the hill, accepted the Coke that had been waiting for him, and marshaled the group. "We might as well go drift down the Nile with baby Noah," he said.

"That's Moses," Debbie informed him.

Ed snapped his fingers. "I knew I was mixed up about something! Sure it wasn't Moses on the Ark?"

"That's Noah," Debbie shouted gleefully. "Let's go to the Ark! There's s'posed to be lots of baby animals there!"

After watching the group out of sight, Shigata asked, "Are you thinking what I'm thinking?"

"I wish I wasn't," Quinn said, "but yes, I am. Did Todd Hansen have anything against Margaret Ruskin? And where was Todd last night and the night before last? Want me to try to find out?"

"Let me think about that," Shigata said. "Because if we do, we're going to have to do it damned quietly."

"We know he knows how to shoot," Quinn said. "Hansen taught him how, years ago. He told us that last year. He'd be able to get a gun if he wanted one, whether Hansen leaves them lying around or not. And he's got the kind of quirky mind that would think it was funny to throw Ruskin to the alligators and Miner to the fish. The only thing is, as best as I can tell he doesn't have any reason."

"Which might not stop him from killing," Shigata said, "if he decided to kill. But these don't look like random killings. Somebody had a reason—whether it was Todd or anybody else. Here comes Joel Moran."

"It took him long enough," Quinn said, watching the medical examiner's investigator approach.

"Damn it, there's got to be some connection," Shigata said, pouring pepper sauce on the collard greens he was still attempting to learn to like.

"Some connection to what?" Quinn asked. "Thanks, Milly," he said over his shoulder, as Milly Horan put a plate of barbecue in front of him.

"Some connection between Ruskin and ArkPark. We know Miner was haunting ArkPark, but why Ruskin? She didn't just accidentally wind up dead there. There was a reason for that location."

"You've said that two dozen times," Quinn observed.

"I'll probably say it two dozen more times. Hi, Steve."

Hansen pulled up a chair. "Dead-endsville," he announced. "Ralph was in Minimax buying carrots about five thirty. He told the checker he was supposed to have been in court today and forgot about it and he had to go call his lawyer and find out what he ought to do about it. The lawyer never heard from him, and I can't find anybody who saw him after that."

"How come the checker remembered the carrots?" Shigata asked.

Hansen made a face. "Because Ralph bought all the carrots in the store—forty pounds—and complained because there weren't more. The checker suggested he try Safeway, but I can't find anybody who remembers him getting there."

"What eats carrots besides Ralph Miner?" Quinn asked. "And horses and mules and hippos?"

"I figure he was going back to ArkPark," Hansen said, agreeing with the thought Quinn hadn't expressed. "But I can't find anybody who saw him get there."

Jack Horan, not waiting for an order, slid a plate in front of Hansen. "Don't you ever get tired of eating exactly the same thing all the time?" Shigata asked.

"No," Hansen said. "It saves me the trouble of having to think about what I'm going to eat. Then I can use my brain for other things."

"No wonder you stay skinny, if food bores you that much," Quinn said. "What other things?"

"Thinking."

"You still trying to dismantle or deconstruct or whatever it was?"

"Yep," Hansen said.

"It still doesn't make a hill of beans of sense to me," Quinn said.

"Doesn't have to, as long as it does to me," Hansen retorted.

"Steve, it doesn't make sense to me either," Shigata said. "I've read about it, in newsmagazines and stuff like that, and from all I can tell it's about proving that things aren't about what they're about. Like—like *Moby-Dick* is about the patriarchy instead of about obsession, and Emily Dickinson's poetry was about masturbation instead of about the entire human condition."

"Not exactly," Hansen said. "The whole idea of aboutness is problematical right now."

"Speak English," Quinn suggested.

"I mean you can't say anything is necessarily about anything, even if the writer thought it was about something specific. The writer has no more right to say what it's about than any educated reader, and sometimes the writer is just plain wrong about what it's about."

"Why would the writer not know what he meant by what he wrote?" Shigata inquired.

"Maybe the writer had repressed something and his subconscious was putting it in the text—or subtext, or course. Or maybe the writer's whole *culture* had repressed something and it was finding its way into the subtext. I'm not saying deconstruction is the way to find out all there is about anything, because it's not. It's *a* way to look at a text, not *the* way to look at a text."

"That sounds like crap to me," Quinn said. "Anyway, what does that have to do with crime scenes? They're not 'about' anything but the crime."

"Aren't they?" Hansen asked. "I think they're 'about' all the reasons, conscious or subconscious, for that particular crime. But anyway, deconstruction isn't about aboutness. It's—it's about—" He paused.

After a moment, Quinn said, "Well? Cat got your tongue?"

"It's sort of about exclusions. Exceptions. What's not said because it's so assumed it never has to be said, and what's not said because it's so—so nonexistent in the mental universe that nobody would think to say it. What seems to be the center and isn't. What seems to be peripheral and is really the center but it looks peripheral because it's so basic nobody ever notices it's the center. And that does apply to crimes."

"Damned if I see how," Quinn said, buttering a biscuit.

"Okay, about twelve years ago there was this Hispanic prostitute murdered in town. Remember that?"

"Vaguely," Quinn said. "I was still in oil field security then." Despite his dubious feeling bout Hansen's theory, he was clearly paying attention.

"Obviously I don't," Shigata said. "I was still with the Bureau. Twelve years ago, I'd have been in Chicago."

"Anyhow, she was a big strong girl—you know, so many Hispanic women are real small, fragile, but she wasn't, and the guy that killed her really wasn't quite as big as she was. They'd fought all over the room. Broken-down bed, torn-off false eyelashes, broken fingernails, you name it. And she was hard to kill. We could see bruises and lumps on her forehead where he'd tried to bash her head in—found out later, at the autopsy, that the only reason he hadn't succeeded was she'd had rickets as a child and her skull was about twice as thick as anybody else's. He'd stuffed towels into the toilet to stop it up and filled it with water. We found her wedged into a small space between the toilet and the wall; her hair was still wet, and we figured he'd drowned her. Well, that was a heavy murder, and you know what our crime scene facilities here are like; they were about ten times worse twelve years ago. I was an investigator then, and I called Galveston—Shipp okayed it—and the Galveston ident people came up to help. Man, we collected every scrap of evidence at that scene. Everything in that room. Fingernails, false eyelashes, a pillow he'd apparently tried to smother her with—the Coke cans and whisky bottles they'd been drinking from, because we figured they'd have his fingerprints on them—we didn't know yet who he was; we found out the next day. Anyway, there was only one thing in that room we didn't bother to collect."

"Which was?" Shigata asked.

"A panty hose package, torn open and sitting on the dresser. It wasn't evidence. There was a pair of snagged panty hose in an overturned trash can and a pair of obviously unused panty hose on the dresser beside the package. We figured she'd opened them and was getting ready to put them on when the fight started. There was no reason he'd ever have touched them. So that was the exception. Everything else in the room was evidence, but that wasn't. We figured it hadn't been involved in the fight . . . and two days later, by the time the medical examiner told us she'd been strangled with a pair of panty hose rather than drowned, that package, and the panty hose, were somewhere in the landfill."

"Shit," Quinn said.

"Yeah. Shit. We traced the guy to Oklahoma. Once he knew we had him, he talked pretty freely. He said he was sorry, he didn't want to kill her, but he was too drunk to get it up. She hadn't laughed at him, but he was afraid she might laugh at him later, and maybe tell other people, if he didn't shut her mouth permanently. He'd tried—as we guessed—to bash her head in, but she was too hardheaded. He'd tried to smother her, but she fought too hard. He'd tried to drown her, but he couldn't get her face into the toilet. And he wound up opening the package of panty hose while she was semi-conscious, strangling her with them, and then unwrapping them from around her neck and dropping them back on the dresser beside the package. The one thing we didn't look at, the one thing that looked peripheral. The exception. And really it was central, and we'd have guessed that if we'd just—deconstructed the crime scene."

"But that's not what usually happens," Shigata objected. "Most of the time what looks central to an investigation really is central and what looks peripheral really is peripheral."

"Maybe that's true," Hansen said. "And maybe our assumption that that's true is one of the reasons why a good sixty percent of all crimes in this country—and around the world, for that matter—go uncleared. Because we're mistaking the central for the peripheral and the peripheral for the central. We're not noticing the exceptions."

"Buddy, I got news for you," Quinn said softly. "There ain't no exception to death."

"Because I said so," Shigata said, an hour later in the muster room, sorting paper and reading the reports, what reports anybody had managed to find time to make.

"Oh, shit!" Hansen said. "You know a lot more about that kind of proceeding than I do."

"R.H.I.P.," Shigata said. "Anyway, you're the one who's looking for central and peripheral ideas and so forth."

"Okay, okay," Hansen said. "Look through the city council minutes back four years, to when ArkPark was first proposed, to see any connections, favorable or otherwise, between Ruskin and ArkPark or between Ralph Miner and ArkPark or between Ruskin and Ralph Miner. Look through four years' worth of Galveston newspapers, ditto. Anything else?"

"That ought to take you a day or two," Shigata said. "After that, we'll see." He turned to Quinn.

"I just talked to Ed on the phone," Quinn said. "He got home about noon, after taking everybody else home. He says Gail is still shook up."

"I'd be surprised if she weren't," Shigata replied. "But Melissa will know how to take care of her, better than I would."

"Ed says he thinks he can get a job at ArkPark. Want him to?"

"Do you?"

"Hell, no," Quinn said. "But that wasn't the question."

"I don't have a right to risk your son's life," Shigata said. "If he wants to get a job at ArkPark just to have a job at ArkPark, that's one thing. But he doesn't have any business trying to nose around."

"He wants a job to save for his mission," Quinn said.

"For his what?" Shigata asked blankly.

Quinn blushed slightly. "Mormon kids—most boys, some girls—go on missions. Only Johnny didn't because he married Mei Ling instead—he would have waited, he did want to go on a mission, only Mei Ling was here on a student visa, and she was scared to go home because her brother was killed in the Tiananmen massacre, so Johnny married her to make sure she was able to stay here. And Steve hasn't decided if he wants to go on one or not, because he's got a scholarship at College of the Mainland and he doesn't know whether they'll hold it till he gets back. So Ed says he's got to go, for the honor of the family. That's what he said, just a couple of weeks ago. I told him that was a funny way to look at it, and he said he couldn't help that. Anyhow—missions—they cost money. The kid and the family together are supposed to pay for it. So Ed wants a job to save for his mission. And ArkPark pays better than anything else he's likely to find around here. He also says—I told him not to try to nose around. There's already two people dead. But he said he can keep his ears open without being too conspicuous."

"Tell him I said not to stick his neck out," Shigata said.

"I already told him not to stick his neck out," Quinn answered. "But he's a kid."

"And he's your son," Hansen said.

Quinn turned to look at him. "I don't know how to take that."

"You can take it as a compliment," Hansen said brusquely. "That boy of mine's got no guts and no character, and I'm damned if I know what to do about it." He headed out the door, shutting it noisily behind himself.

"I don't know what to tell him," Quinn said. "Ed's right, of course, on part of what the boy needs, but I don't think Hansen knows how to give it to him."

"Let me toss out a suggestion," Shigata said. "See if you can get Ed to talk Todd into going with him to get a job at ArkPark. Summer's coming on, and he'll probably be wanting a job. If you can get him more under Ed's influence, and less under the influence of those jerks he runs around with—"

"That's worth a try," Quinn agreed. "But what makes you think he'll listen to Ed? Or did you forget Ed just punched him out today?"

"That's why he'll listen to Ed," Shigata said. "Nobody else—at least from his point of view—cares enough about what he does to punch him out. My guess is that whether he'll admit it or not, he's glad Ed does."

"That makes sense," Quinn said. "What else do you want me to do now? I mean in terms of trying to find out who slew Lew? That is, after all, what we're supposed to be doing, not teaching Todd Hansen manners. Which for my money is as like as not to be impossible anyway. I don't know, maybe I'm wrong. I hope I am. But I don't want to bet on it."

Shigata took a deep breath. "Go talk to Ed," he said. "See if he can get Todd talking. Find out where Todd was the last two nights. It's a sure thing Hansen doesn't know."

"Why not?"

"Barndt was off duty." No more, he felt, needed to be said. Sergeant Steve Hansen apparently believed nobody knew he was sleeping with Corporal Claire Barndt. Everybody else—including Barndt—knew everybody knew it.

"I know," Quinn said. "But she went to Dallas for her cousin's wedding."

"In that case," Shigata answered, "Hansen might know where his son was those two nights."

Quinn chuckled, and Shigata went on. "After you've talked to Ed, go see if you can get a line on where Miner went after he left Minimax."

"What makes you think I can find out something Hansen can't?" Quinn remained sensitive over his lack of education, relative to Hansen's and Shigata's.

"You're not emotionally involved with where Miner went, and he is. Besides that, you and I both know you've got a lot more people smarts than Hansen does."

Quinn stood up. "I'll see what I can do. What are you going to be doing?"

"I'm going back out and talk with Ruskin's tenants

again," Shigata said. "I figure we've got more questions to ask than we did yesterday."

Irene Athanasopoulous—"Don't try to pronounce it," she told Shigata, "nobody around here does except that Quinn boy, and he just does it to show off"—was an angry woman. "My husband isn't home," she said. "He cooks on one of those offshore drilling rigs, so he's home a week and then gone two weeks, but if he was here he would tell you the same thing I'm telling you."

She energetically dusted off the coffee table, which had not a speck of dust on it. The house, small and shabby as it was, was spotlessly clean. "Mrs. Ruskin was a spiteful woman. There was *no* other reason except spite for her to take me in and show me that poor Evans girl's house when she hadn't had time to clean it up. I wouldn't have taken this place, I wouldn't stay here for a minute, except it was the cheapest thing we could find besides that garage apartment which was just flat too little, and we're trying to save up to buy a restaurant. George got out of the navy three months ago, and we're living on his retirement and saving every penny he makes on the drilling rig, and every penny I make at Denny's—I'm a waitress on the midnight shift—so that we can have our own place. Even Junior's excited about getting our own place; he's putting half of what he makes into the fund—he can't put everything in, of course, because he's buying a car and he has dates and stuff like that, but he's doing what he can, because of course whatever we get, it'll be his someday."

"Junior's your son?"

She nodded. "He's nineteen. A good, hardworking boy."

"Where does he work?"

"ArkPark," she said. "He'd been working at Denny's—a busboy, but of course you have to start somewhere—so he could learn the restaurant business, but he decided to go to work at ArkPark instead because the pay was a lot better. And, too, Reverend Hobby is so nice to the kids. He really seems to care."

"How long has Junior worked for ArkPark? I guess that's a silly question, considering it just opened—"

"He was with it a long time before that," she said. "He helped with the construction, so actually—let's see, I guess he's been with them for two years or so, since right after he got out of high school."

"Now I'm confused about timing, Mrs. Ath—"

"Just call me Irene," she interrupted. "I know, because I told you we were hunting for a place because my husband just got out of the navy. But Junior and I were living with my sister and her son in Texas City the last couple of years George was in the navy, because he was on sea duty, and it just happened that my sister got married—second marriage, of course—just about the time he was discharged, so of course George and I wanted a place of our own, which of course we would have done anyway, but it made it a lot easier that Helen wasn't going to feel hurt about me moving out." She paused, apparently for breath. "Of course, this doesn't have anything to do with what you want to know, except of course that Junior works at ArkPark and Mrs. Ruskin was killed there, but that doesn't have anything to do with Junior and of course hundreds of people work at ArkPark."

"What time does Junior get home?" Shigata asked.

"Why do you want to know that?"

"He might have some ideas I wouldn't, since he knows ArkPark so well."

Lynette Evans wasn't home. That was predictable; she was a secretary. Nor was anybody home at the Gonzaleses' apartment. Mei Ling Quinn was home; she was shy, and pretty, and her English was difficult for Shigata to understand.

She was wearing the ivory bracelet Quinn had mentioned, and he was right—except for its obvious age, it appeared identical to the one in Margaret Ruskin's purse and the one in the toilet tank. Shigata asked her about it. "It belong to my grandmother," she said, putting her hand on it protectively. "My mother hide it, during the wars. I bring it to

America. Not wear; too old, too easy break. But I wear all the time now."

"Why's that?" Shigata asked.

"Someone steal my grandmother's things. Grandmother's spirit very sad, I very sad. Then bring back. I find in mailbox. I not want someone steal again."

Shigata took the plastic bags out of his briefcase and spread them in front of her. "Have you ever seen these?" he asked.

She looked at them, her eyes wide. Then she stood up, left the room for a moment. She returned with ivory hairpins and an ivory necklace and set them beside the plastic bags. Except for the age, the old ivory and the new ivory were identical. "They steal to copy?"

"Maybe," Shigata said.

She picked up the plastic bags and then put them down dismissingly. "Mine hand-carve," she said. "Craftsman. Take a long time. These—too alike. Too alike made with machine. How make with machine?"

"I don't know," Shigata said. "Where were your grandmother's things stolen from?"

"Pardon?"

"Where did you keep your grandmother's things, before they were stolen?"

She didn't answer for a moment. Then she asked, "You not laugh?"

"I promise not to laugh."

"Government in Beijing not want people keep grandmother's things. We hide. Different places, different times. When I come to America I hide in—in—" She blushed. "In Kotex box," she got out with some difficulty. "Nobody look there. Nobody but me."

"And that's where they were stolen from?"

She nodded. "I at school. Johnny at work. Somebody look in box. Very strange place to look, even for burglar."

Shigata was inclined to agree.

Unless it was a female burglar.

Margaret Ruskin being nosy? Or—somebody else?

Were they stolen to be copied? If so, how had the thief known where to look for them?

Or were they stolen for another reason, maybe found by accident, by a thief looking for something else, and then the thief—or someone the thief knew—decided to copy them?

Whichever the reason was, why had the thief returned them?

What was central, and what was peripheral?

Chapter 5

"WHY SHOULD I?" Todd asked, his customary sullen appearance slightly mitigated by curiosity.

"So you'll have some spending money you don't have to ask your dad for. So you won't be bored all summer, the way you are evenings and weekends and the way you were last summer. And, frankly, to keep you out of trouble. Is that enough, or do you need more reasons?"

"How do you know we'll get the jobs?"

"I don't," Ed said patiently. "But I know they're hiring and we've got as good a chance as anybody else. I've heard Hobby prefers kids who are making good grades in school, and that's one thing we're both doing."

"There shouldn't be any problem," the receptionist said smoothly, handing them both applications. "We're really still terribly shorthanded, even with the wonderful help that comes from Reverend Hobby's homeless shelter in Galveston." Her tone of voice, and the expression on her face, did not match the enthusiasm in her words, and Ed found himself wondering how helpful the people from the shelter really were. Some, of course, would be perfectly capable, willing, and eager to go to work, but without a job to do, and they—provided they were fed well enough to rebuild strength lost

through protracted malnutrition—should be useful in this
or any other work. But there was always a certain percentage
of the homeless who were mentally ill, dumped back on the
streets by a system that had decided the warehousing of the
mentally ill was inhumane, and there was always a certain
percentage who were hopeless alcoholics or drug addicts.
Ed had heard enough discussion of this sort of problem at
home to be fairly realistic about it, despite the optimism
of youth.

"You'll need to bring either copies of your most recent
report cards or notes from your school," the receptionist
added, "before we can put you to work on more than a pro-
visional basis. Reverend Hobby won't hire teenagers who are
failing in school; he feels they should be working on their
grades."

"Makes sense," Ed agreed, glancing over the employment
form. "But we're both fine."

"Well, I'm glad to hear that." She continued to hover over
them, and Ed wondered if there was something else she
wanted to say and couldn't figure out how. He would be the
first to admit that he and Todd Hansen made an odd-looking
pair. Like his father and mother, Ed Quinn was short, no
more than five-five and probably now at his full growth;
again like his parents, he was inclined to be chunky, although so far the extra weight was more muscle than fat.
The black hair and brown eyes of his Vietnamese mother
topped a light, almost delicate, café au lait complexion. Todd
Hansen had his father's height—six-four now and probably
not through growing—and his mother's coloring, hair so fair
it was almost white, blue eyes. He was probably, genetically,
meant to be lean, but laziness and overeating had put a beer
belly on him already, and his skin had a pasty cast rather
than the healthy fairness of his parents.

"It's nice to see friends come out together to hunt work,"
the receptionist continued too heartily. "I'll try to see to it
we have you working close together."

That, Ed could easily have done without, except for the
fact that he was trying to keep an eye on Todd. He didn't

like Todd Hansen. To the best of his knowledge, nobody liked Todd Hansen. It wasn't that Todd was intrinsically unlikable; rather, it seemed that Todd went out of his way—at times, considerably out of his way—to annoy people.

But like him or not, Ed was stuck with him for a while. He began to fill out the employment application, only partially aware of Todd beside him doing the same.

The door to an inner office opened, and an extremely neat-looking middle-aged man in a gray business suit emerged. He paused, looking at Ed and Todd, frowning slightly. Then, abruptly, he said, "The two of you were in the group who discovered—ah—Mr. Miner's body."

Ed looked up, surprised. "Yes, sir, we were. But I didn't see you there."

The man smiled. "I wasn't. But I didn't have to be. Come and let me show you something."

"Something" was a room down the hall. The door, marked "security," opened into a normal-looking office with desks and file cabinets. But, at the touch of a button, three walls slid into the floor, to reveal three interior walls full of video monitor screens. Each one showed a different perspective of ArkPark—the alligator pit and the Red Sea diorama along with virtually everything else. "Then you saw the murders take place," Ed blurted.

The man smiled. "No, I'm sorry to say, neither I nor anyone else saw the murders take place. We have an extensive security staff, of course, but the only people trusted to know even of the existence of this room are myself—"

"And who are you?" Todd interrupted.

"Clifford Hobby," the man said, in an of-course tone that seemed to question the necessity for any such inquiry. He then continued, "Myself and two highly trusted staff members, one of whom customarily monitors at night and one of whom customarily monitors in the afternoon, those being the two times when vandalism is most likely. Mornings tend to be relatively trouble free. The room is not covered at all times, you see, but in such matters a random pattern is normally quite as useful as full-time coverage."

Ed, who'd heard discussion of random patrol patterns at home, nodded; Todd only looked puzzled.

"The night that poor Mrs. Ruskin was killed, the night monitor was out because his sweet wife was giving birth to a baby. He remained out for several more days and in fact has still not returned to work. And, of course, as I said, no one customarily monitors in the morning. Most unfortunate, to be sure, as full-time monitoring would not only have caught the—ah—killer but also have protected you dear children from the shock of finding—ah—of finding the body of poor Mr. Miner." Hobby beamed benignly.

"Did you tell the police about this monitor bank?" Ed asked. At eighteen he did not regard himself as a child, dear or otherwise, and he didn't see how anybody could honestly think of Todd as a dear child either.

"Why no," Hobby said. "Do you think I should?"

"Of course you should," Todd retorted. "Don't you videotape these things?"

"Oh, dear, no," Hobby said. "The cost of that much videotape would be quite prohibitive."

"If this is so secret that most of your staff doesn't know about it," Ed said, "how come you decided to tell us?"

"You are policemen's sons, are you not?" Hobby asked. "Don't tell me I was in error in that belief."

"I very much doubt," Ed said, "that you are in error about much of anything." He didn't mean it as a compliment, and he was fairly sure Hobby took it the way it was meant.

But Hobby was probably used to that kind of reaction. He laughed, lightly and shortly, and then said, in a perfectly suave tone, "You are, of course, here to—ah—shall we say, conduct espionage?"

"What?" Todd said.

"Of course I do not expect you to admit it; a spy who confesses to spying is, at the very least, counterproductive."

"We're here because we want work," Ed said flatly. "I'm one of twelve children, and my mom obviously hasn't got time to have a money-making job. If you think a Bayport police officer has an easy time supporting twelve children, I suggest you think again."

Hobby turned his attention to Todd. "Are you also one of twelve children?" he asked ironically. Todd's spoiled appearance made the question reasonably unnecessary.

"No," Todd said, "but I bore easy. Besides that, if I don't have a job my dad'll make me dig the garden all summer and I hate that."

"I cannot dig; to beg I am ashamed," Hobby said. Todd looked blankly puzzled, but Ed laughed out loud. Hobby, astonished out of his usual blandness, said, "You recognize the quotation?"

"I'm pretty well acquainted with the Bible," Ed said casually. "The parable of the unjust steward." He did not, at least at the moment, see any need to explain that Mormon teenagers—although his father was a recent convert, his mother was not, and all twelve children had been raised in the church—spend an hour a day, five days a week, for the entire four years of high school studying religion, and that those seminary classes include a full year of Old Testament study and a full year of New Testament study. He preferred simply to study Hobby's reaction.

"Well!" Hobby said. "Perhaps I was wrong as to your intentions. But you would not, I assume, be averse to reporting to your fathers anything you might chance to learn here?"

"We would certainly do that," Ed said cautiously, wondering more than ever what Hobby was up to.

"Well, then," Hobby said, "consider that your fathers, through you, are now notified of this interesting room. I shall instruct Evangeline to put you on the security payroll. Drop by my office tomorrow and Evangeline will have keys to this room for you, and you may come in and monitor whenever you wish, although I would prefer that you not actually handle the controls—except of course this button that reveals the screens and this other button that conceals them again—as some of the equipment is quite delicate. And of course you will never leave the screens visible when you depart the room. Wander freely around the park. All parts of it are now open to you. Learn all you can. Someone, clearly, is misusing my facilities in a shocking manner, and it is possible that you can learn something my adult security staff cannot. You will, of course, report to me as well as to your fathers. This type of thing can be most embarrassing to my ministry, and clearing it up is of critical importance to me."

"Yes, I can see that murder might be embarrassing to a television ministry," Ed said. "Of course if we're on your payroll we'll report to you. But I suggest that our presence would be more believable, and therefore less suspicious, if you put us to work in visible areas." He was deliberately sounding as stuffy as possible, and he'd been studying stuffiness, as well as the intended course matter, under the unwitting guidance of a particular high school mathematics teacher.

"Ah, yes," Hobby said. "Evangeline will see to that also. And now you will of course want to go and report to your fathers—"

Outside, Todd said bitterly, "We could have had a cushy spot and now you've got us back shoveling elephant shit!"

"You have to be alive to shovel elephant shit," Ed answered.

"What's that supposed to mean?"

"Every kid our age in town knows who our dads are," Ed said. "Hobby won't be the only one suspicious of us. Todd, get this through your cotton-pickin' thick head. Somebody murdered Mrs. Ruskin and Mr. Miner. Whoever did it thought it was funny. They wouldn't have stuck the bodies where they did if they didn't think it was funny. They'd think it was just as funny to murder us. I don't know about you, but I'd rather shovel elephant shit. I've got a few things I want to accomplish before I die."

Mark Shigata was thinking about Margaret Ruskin's daughter, Amy, and Margaret Ruskin's sister, Moira. He was sure in his own mind that both of them knew things they weren't telling not because they weren't willing to discuss them but because they were unaware that they mattered. Unwillingly, his mind wandered back to Hansen's comments about centrality and peripherality. His head insisted that the whole idea was no more than a crackpot literary theory, being applied to crime by a man Shigata had long since decided wasn't exactly the most practical human being in the whole universe.

But something on the gut level kept insisting that Hansen might, just might, be right. Because it wasn't always obvious what was central and what was peripheral, in anything. If anybody had asked him while the breakup was going on, he'd have said his first marriage collapsed because Wendy, because she had been poor so long, wanted more luxuries than he could provide her and thought he was stingy when he tried to explain to her that there were some things he just couldn't afford. It wasn't until a long time later that he realized that the demand for luxuries was peripheral, in fact so peripheral that it scarcely mattered. What was central was that Wendy had been abused by every man she'd ever known, and because Shigata didn't abuse her she didn't know what to make of him. Her demand for luxuries was in fact a demand that he abuse her, and because he refused to do that she went out hunting a man who would, and, when she found that man, ultimately he murdered her. Good psychiatric help might have solved the problem, but Shigata didn't know that then, and neither did Wendy.

That, of course, was past; there was nothing he could do about it. But now? The murder he was supposed to be investigating? What was central, and what was peripheral? ArkPark—he'd supposed it had to be central, because both bodies were found there, but what if he was wrong? If Ark-Park was peripheral, then what was central?

He'd supposed that the ivory was central, and he'd supposed that it was peripheral, and right now he honestly didn't know.

His guess had been that the fact that Margaret Ruskin was on the city council was central, until Ralph Miner, who certainly wasn't involved in government on the city or any other level, also turned up dead at ArkPark. Now his guess was that the city council membership was peripheral, but he'd sent Hansen to check for the possibility that he was wrong.

His guess was that Ruskin's well-known nosiness was central, and he still thought that, because Miner was also well known for nosiness. So far, in fact, that was the only connection or similarity he had found between the victims.

The fact was that his thoughts so far had been singularly unproductive. Either something was going on at ArkPark and the murders had been there because that was where the problem was, or something was going on somewhere else and the bodies had been left at ArkPark to distract everybody's attention from wherever the real problem was.

Clifford Hobby was, or was not, involved.

Shigata, for reasons he could not begin to define—*I do not like thee, Doctor Fell / The reason why I cannot tell / But this I know and know full well / I do not like thee, Doctor Fell*— did not like Clifford Hobby. But he was well aware that his dislike didn't make Hobby culpable. It proved nothing at all except that Shigata, for reasons perhaps known to his subconscious but not to his conscious mind, did not like overly well dressed men with overly soft hands and overly smoothly manipulative manners.

The one thing Shigata was sure of, or at least as sure as he could reasonably be without having cleared the two murder cases, was that they were related. The chance that two people had been murdered for totally unrelated reasons, and both left at ArkPark within a two-day period, one in a million-gallon fish tank and one in an alligator pit, was virtually nonexistent. But he couldn't find any relationship between the two, other than the obvious fact that both were extremely, and notoriously, fond of minding other people's business, and both were strongly opposed to the building of ArkPark.

There'd been theories, of course—mainly from Hansen, and Shigata was fairly, but not totally, sure that Hansen had been joking. He'd suggested that Miner was Ruskin's illegitimate son, a hypothesis for which there was no evidence whatever and which, even if it was true, would not be a reason for murder, or at least not for these particular murders. He'd also suggested satanic cults, but when Quinn had hooted at that he'd merely shrugged and said, "Well, I don't really think so either."

And probably he didn't. The problem was nobody could think of anything that *did* seem to make sense.

Shigata had a headache. And it was not improved when Ed Quinn and Todd Hansen, both extremely excited, burst into his office and began telling him what they had learned.

Never mind what Al Quinn was supposed to be thinking about. He was, in fact, thinking about carrots. Forty pounds of carrots. Forty pounds of carrots, and a dead man who didn't have a car or truck but who carried a video camera and, apparently, forty pounds of carrots around on a bicycle. An old bicycle, which come to think of it hadn't been located yet.

It was undeniably true that Ralph Miner had possessed an uncanny ability to transport, on that old bicycle, things nobody would ever have imagined could be transported by bicycle, including two large, live, and probably struggling seals, which he had succeeded in carrying nearly twenty miles before dumping them into the water. (There was seawater closer, but it was, he'd said, too polluted for the seals.) He hadn't, of course, had the video camera with him then.

But he had had the video camera with him when he'd bought forty pounds of carrots at Minimax and complained because there weren't more. Hansen hadn't mentioned the camera, but Quinn went back and asked the checker himself and she told him. She'd probably told Hansen too, but he was so used to thinking of Miner and that video camera together he didn't think to mention it to Shigata and Quinn.

That thought, unfortunately, led Quinn back to Hansen's current pet topic. Quinn had dropped out of high school briefly in the ninth grade, returned for a couple of years when he realized he had a choice between going to high school or wrestling with his father's mule, and then dropped out for good to enlist in the army toward the end of the eleventh grade. He wasn't, then, expecting to wind up in Vietnam, much less in a Vietcong prison camp.

But he wasn't stupid, and Hansen's explanation, about things that are never mentioned because they are so much a part of the culture or situation that they go without saying, and things that are never mentioned because they are so foreign to the culture or situation that they are unimaginable, made sense. All that didn't make sense was, first, why Hansen hadn't thought to apply the theory to himself and realize Shigata and Quinn needed to know *all* he knew about Miner, and, second, what in the heck the theory had to do with crime, and especially with crime scenes, anyway.

Mainly, though, he was thinking about carrots. What would anybody, even Ralph Miner, do with forty pounds of carrots? Probably he was going to ArkPark, but even he, with his wild suggestions of animal abuse, had no reason to suppose the animals at ArkPark were not being fed. On the contrary, it was quite evident—witness the tons of hippo poop that Junior Ath-whatever-his-name-was was offering to sell—that the animals were being quite well fed.

So what would you do with forty pounds of carrots?

If you wanted to distract the attention of a dog, you might give it a hunk of beef. If you wanted to distract the attention of an ape—something Quinn had heard wasn't as easy as it was popularly supposed to be—you might give it a bunch of bananas. It seemed fairly reasonable to assume that the forty pounds of carrots were intended to distract the attention of some animal or group of animals. But which? And why?

What animals eat carrots? To the best of Quinn's knowledge, just about any nonmeat-eating animal, from tortoises and bunnies, whose attention wouldn't need to be distracted, to elephants, who wouldn't be distracted very long by forty pounds of carrots.

Like Hansen, Quinn hadn't been able to trace Miner past Minimax, and he'd checked every store, and every restaurant, in Bayport and also in LaMarque and Texas City. He was out of ideas. Right now he wanted to go in and talk with Shigata.

* * *

If Steve Hansen had needed any reminder about why a man with a Ph.D. from the University of Texas was working as a cop instead of a scholar, he'd just gotten it. Looking things up, when you have a pretty good idea what you're after, are reasonably interested, and have at least halfway decent indexes, is one thing. Spending hours digging through disorganized files, not knowing what you're looking for except that it might involve the name of one or more of three individuals, is something else entirely.

He'd rigged a makeshift desk in the same dusty city records storeroom in which he'd hidden after breaking out of prison, setting the papers he was looking through on top of the very same old tax record box in which he'd once hidden a pistol, a holster, a sleeping bag, and a thousand dollars in change and small bills. He'd looked through ten years of city legal records and ten years of city commission records, and found exactly nothing to link Ralph Miner, Margaret Ruskin, and/or Clifford Hobby. His hands were blackened with old dust, he'd been coughing off and on for the last two hours, and he was too disgusted even to think about deconstruction. Mainly he wanted a drink, to clear the dust out of his throat, and although it was now after four, which put him officially off duty, he was well aware that he couldn't either depart or have a drink until he'd reported to Shigata on what he had, or in this case hadn't, learned.

So he guessed he'd better go talk with Shigata.

He didn't have to go around the front of the building; one of the areas this storeroom opened into was the back of the police station. So he went that way, and was glad he had done so, because he heard the commotion in the muster room before he was more than two feet into the hall.

He should have realized—and probably would have, if he'd thought about it—that although murder is so commonplace it rarely makes the back pages of most big-city newspapers anymore, these murders were somewhat less than commonplace. Margaret Ruskin had been fairly newsworthy; Ralph Miner had made himself somewhat newsworthy; and the murders themselves were, to say the least, unusual.

The reporters had come from Houston, Galveston, Austin, even Dallas and Fort Worth, and Shigata, holding them at bay, didn't look happy. The first thing Hansen heard, even before he saw Shigata or the reporters, was Shigata's voice saying, "We don't know yet."

"Well, what is the connection between Miner and Ark-Park?" a reporter shouted.

"Mr. Miner was arrested several months ago for stealing seals before ArkPark opened," Shigata said, "and releasing them in the Gulf. Other than that, I don't know of a connection."

"Is it true that he was in ArkPark the day before his body was found?"

"Yes—"

Hansen decided he'd heard enough. If he let them see him, he figured, they'd start asking him questions too. So he slipped past the door to the muster room, passing behind Shigata and hoping reporters wouldn't notice him behind the half-closed door to the hall, and ducked into the locker room, where he found Quinn. "You hiding too?" he asked.

"You better believe it," Quinn said. "Those are jackals out there. Hyenas. That's one of the reasons I wouldn't want his job."

"You got more?"

"How many do you want? Not that they'd hire me for anything like that anyway. They would you. Would you be a chief of police, if you could?"

"Are you kidding?" Hansen said. "Not on your life. I wouldn't have it if they offered it to me. I like my peace and quiet too much."

"You and me both."

The door to the locker room opened. "You can both come out now," Shigata said. "They're gone."

"How'd you know we were in here?" Quinn asked, sounding a little embarrassed.

"I heard you both sneak by," Shigata said. "Day watch

has gone home, and evening watch is on the street. There's nobody still here but us."

"So you won't mind if we go home too," Hansen said.

"I won't mind," Shigata returned, "after I've heard what you have to say."

But the three were still talking in the chief's office when the dispatcher called on the intercom. "A Mr. Hobby is here and wants to talk with you."

"Okay," Shigata said. "Give me a minute."

"I'm leaving," Quinn announced.

"Damn intercoms you can overhear," Shigata said. "No you're not leaving. Sit back down. We're all going to hear this. Hansen, go bring him in here. *Without* laughing."

"You may be asking the impossible," Hansen said. "The guy is so damned comical." But he assumed a sober face and ambled out the door.

"Why do you want me to stay?" Quinn asked. "I don't have anything to say to that blasphemous son of a bitch. Putting a diorama of Gethsemane in the middle of an amusement park—"

"You don't have to say anything," Shigata answered. "The way you feel, I'd rather you didn't. All I want you to do is listen. Remember, he may be sincere. He may feel that if you can't attract kids to churches you take religious ideas to where kids are. Try to listen with an open mind, and see what kind of feeling you get. "

Hansen returned, escorting the Reverend Clifford Hobby. "Have a seat," Shigata said. "Hansen, will you get a—"

Hansen was already hauling an extra chair in from the adjacent muster room, and Hobby seated himself. Either he was wearing the same suit he had been wearing yesterday, Shigata judged, or else he had a fairly good supply of gray silk suits. "What can we do for you?" Shigata asked.

"Did—ah—the boys, I suppose I should say the young men, report to you about—"

"The bank of television monitors? Yes, I was just telling Captain Quinn and Sergeant Hansen about them," Shigata said. "Is there any special reason why you didn't tell us about them sooner?"

"I—ah—" Hobby wiped his brow. "I suppose it didn't really occur to me that they were relevant. After poor Mrs. Ruskin was murdered—of course nobody was manning the monitors then—I assumed that was a freak occurrence that probably would never be repeated. If—ah—if I had told you then, would it have helped?"

Shigata thought about it. Would he, really, have ordered somebody to man those monitors if he had known about them? If he had done so, would that monitoring necessarily have saved Ralph Miner's life, or even helped in locating his killer? The question was moot, because Shigata was reasonably certain he, too, would have assumed Ruskin's murder to be a freak occurrence. He would not have ordered the monitors manned. "No," he said, "it probably wouldn't have made any difference. But you really should have told us this morning, after it became clear that the first murder *wasn't* that unrepeatable freak situation we all thought it was."

"I should have," Hobby agreed. "I—ah—watched, on the monitor, after my office was notified of the finding of the body. Watched your investigation, I mean. I—ah—was trying to decide whether to tell you or not. I was afraid you would think that I had—ah—deliberately kept the information from you earlier, when in fact I—ah—simply hadn't thought of telling you."

"So at that point you were deliberately keeping the information from us," Shigata said bluntly.

"I—ah—" Hobby was sweating visibly. "I—yes, I suppose I was. Temporarily. I would have told you. I intended to; I was just—ah—pondering the best way to go about it. Then the young men came in, and I took that as a God-given opportunity to—ah—atone for past errors."

"I'm glad that you came in to talk with us," Shigata said, "because I would have been telephoning you shortly if you hadn't. We're going to need to put someone in to monitor that screen tonight."

"That won't be necessary," Hobby protested. "The—ah—

my security man, Burton Wells, a very competent young man indeed, who normally monitors the screen at night, has returned to work."

"I'm sure you can understand my preference for having someone of my own there too," Shigata said.

"Well, now that you put it that way, yes, of course I can understand—"

"How late does Mr. Wells normally work?" Shigata interrupted.

"Ah—he normally comes on duty at ten P.M. and works until six in the morning."

"And you also have an afternoon monitor?"

"Ah—yes. From two P.M. until ten P.M. Glenn Wells."

"Any relation?"

"To Burton? Yes, they're brothers. They were—ah—in the process of setting up a security firm of their own, when I hired them to jointly run security at ArkPark."

"So your actual head of security—coheads, I should say—monitors these screens?"

"That is correct," Hobby said.

Shigata thought a moment. He was almost certain that if something to trigger murder at ArkPark was happening it would not begin until the park was cleared of extraneous people. "What time does the park close to visitors?"

"We close the gates at ten thirty," Hobby said. "We shut down the rides and the snack bars at eleven. Most visitors depart by—ah—call it eleven fifteen, when they find there is nothing further for them to do."

"Then we'll have a police officer there about ten," Shigata said, "to monitor as the last people leave, and we'll keep one there all night."

"I—ah—suppose I should be grateful. After all, someone is clearly attempting to discredit my ministry in the most appalling manner possible, and by finding out who that person is you will be—ah—aiding me greatly. I shall notify both Glenn and Burton to expect your representative. And who will that be?"

Shigata had Patrolman Paul Ames in mind, but before he

could open his mouth to say so, Quinn said, "Me."

Hobby looked at him. "Sergeant Quinn, I have had the—ah—the distinct impression that you disapprove of Ark-Park."

"I do," Quinn said. "If you want to know the truth, I don't think anybody could discredit your ministry more than you've done yourself. You've turned a religion that means a lot to me into a carnival act, and that makes me furious. I don't like you and I don't like ArkPark. But that's no reason for murder."

Chapter 6

THERE WAS A LOT of work that could still be done, and Shigata always felt guilty leaving work at all when he was investigating a murder. But he knew he wasn't Superman, and he had been working ten to fourteen hours a day for the last week. He couldn't keep that pace up permanently. Like it or not, he was only one man, and if another murder happened while he was still trying to clear these two, it wouldn't be his fault, no matter how much it might—and would—feel as if it were. But there was one more thing he had to finish before he took off.

It had occurred to him that the videotape in Miner's camera, if it could be salvaged, would certainly tell the last thing Miner had photographed, and might well provide at least a clue about what he had been doing that had caused someone to decide to kill him.

Shigata knew he wasn't competent to deal with the videotape. The FBI lab could do it, but, constantly overloaded as the technicians there were, they might take two or three months to get to it. A phone call to the Texas crime lab in Austin hadn't helped; nobody there had ever had to cope with videotape that had been soaked overnight in seawater.

There is a theory—and Shigata had tested it before—that if you do your homework before you start calling, you should be able to lay your hands on any fact in the world, provided it is neither a government secret nor a proprietary trade secret, in a maximum of five telephone calls. Shigata figured the same theory should apply to locating the right expert.

It took four calls. The first place Shigata called—a store that put home movies on videotape—didn't have anybody who seemed to know anything. At the second place, which offered the same service, a woman said, "I don't do it myself, but if you call Evan Rogers—" She gave him the phone number.

Evan Rogers didn't do it, but he suggested Chester Stratford. And Chester Stratford, it developed, was the expert Shigata had been hunting. Rescuing water-soaked videotape wasn't his normal job—he was a professional nature photographer who lived in Galveston—but he'd had to rescue his own tape often enough that he'd gotten pretty good at it, and, according to his wife, he'd helped out the Coast Guard a couple of times lately when video cameras had gotten soaked. He was at present, also according to his wife, out walking on the beach. That was better than Shigata had expected; considering his work, the man could just as well have been in Zanzibar or Tanganyika—well, Tanzania. Was there a number where he could call back, she asked. Because if there was—

After leaving his home telephone number, Shigata called it a day.

Melissa—lately he'd begun calling her Lissa, which she seemed to like—met him at the front door, finger to her lips, with an eloquent glance at the couch. Gail was asleep, half-covered by a white crocheted throw. The cat the Quinns had given her was curled by her head, purring lustily, obviously delighted to have his girl all to himself at such an unusual hour.

Shigata followed Lissa into the kitchen, carefully closing the door to the darkened living room. "Is she sick?" he asked.

"You may be used to seeing bodies," Lissa said, a little tartly. "She isn't. Mark, she's fifteen and she thinks she's grown up, but this kind of thing—she's still a child. She cried for two hours after she got home. She was hysterical, I mean really hysterical. I finally called the doctor and he said she was probably a little bit shocky and called in a prescription—Valium, for a few days, until she calms down."

"I knew she was upset," Shigata said, "but I figured you'd know better what to do about that than I would. I did talk to her, before the kids left the park, but she was putting up a tough-guy act then."

"Of course. Her friends were there." Lissa still sounded angry—to Shigata, unreasonably angry, and he didn't know whether to be delighted because this was the first time she'd let him see anger, or furious because she was blaming him for something he hadn't caused and couldn't help.

"Look," he said, "I didn't know she was going to ArkPark to find a corpse. If I'd known I wouldn't have let her go. Obviously."

"Obviously," Lissa agreed. "But there was a body there yesterday—"

"That didn't, for cryin' out loud, mean I had any reason to expect to find a body there today." He was trying not to lose his temper, but he could hear his voice rising.

"Mark, I'm not trying to pick a fight with you." Her voice also was rising.

"Okay," he said. "Okay. I know you're not. It's just—it's been a hell of a day, for all of us. Don't try to cook anything. When Gail wakes up we'll go out for dinner. If she looks like sleeping through the night, I'll go bring in a pizza or something. Right now I'm going out to work in the garden for a few minutes. I'm expecting an important phone call, though, so—"

"If it comes I'll call you in." She sounded a little subdued.

Normally he changed clothes before heading for the garden—jeans and a chambray shirt, the kind of clothes he'd learned from Quinn, with the inevitable pistol at his hip because when the police department needed him when he was off duty it needed him fast. But he found working in the garden relaxing, and right now he definitely needed some kind of relaxation.

His slacks were washable, and he'd conformed enough, now, to the South Texas ethos that he almost never wore a suit or jacket anymore. If he had to go back out, he'd arrive with dirt on his slacks and shirt, but if they needed to call him in after he'd left for the day, the dirt wouldn't matter, probably wouldn't be noticed at all.

This was the third year he'd put the garden in this same spot, where he'd torn down an old garage the year Wendy was murdered. He didn't let himself dwell on what had happened to him in that garage, before he'd finished pulling it down. That was past; that was over. The spot was a garden now.

It was too late, too hot, for radishes, or cabbage, and very few people ever attempted to grow lettuce this far south. The corn was four feet high, and squash and beans sprawled in a thicket at the base of the corn, simultaneously collecting sun for themselves and cooling the ground the way the corn liked it. Cucumbers rambled over what was left of a fence, partially removed now, that had separated the garage from the house. Tomatoes and peppers were covered with flowers and small green fruit, and the marigolds planted between them blazed with orange and yellow. Shigata clipped off a few fading flower heads, to encourage the blossoms to continue, and pulled a couple of weeds and tossed them onto the path, to be transferred later to the compost heap.

It was about time to plant more green beans. He tried to plant a row every two or three weeks, to keep the beans going until late fall, which, this close to the Gulf of Mexico, came very late indeed.

The ground was still soft from the last time he'd rototilled it. He built up the row with his hand, pulling soil into place, feeling for roots of weeds that might have escaped the tilling and tossing them, too, out onto the path. A wide double row. The seed packets were safe from rodents, inside an old glass pickle jar on a shelf of the garden shed he and Quinn had built last summer. He got the bean packet out, screwed one of the three metal wheels onto the Garden Weasel, and dug two small trenches in the top of the row.

By now he could feel his tension beginning to evaporate. He dropped the seeds into the trenches, spacing them carefully, firming the soil over them, and then went to unroll the hose to water them in.

Lissa, at the door, called, "Mark!"

"What is it?" he answered, pausing with the hose in his hand. "Telephone? Tell them just a minute. My hands are dirty."

"No, not the telephone, but Gail's awake."

"Send her out here."

He went on unrolling the hose, set the nozzle to the lightest spray possible, and turned the water on. When Gail came out the door, he was spraying water onto the newly planted bean patch. He watched her pause briefly, just outside, before threading her way through the feathery plumes of carrots—maybe he had planted just a few too many different things, for a yard this size—to come on out to where he was. "Feeling pretty crummy?" he asked conversationally.

She nodded and watched him a few moments. "The first tomatoes are going to be ready to pick in a few days."

"Looks that way," he agreed.

"If we had a greenhouse, we could have fresh tomatoes all year round."

"That's true."

"It could be just a little greenhouse," she said. "We could put it beside my room."

"Possibly we could."

There was a long silence. Shigata rinsed the dirt off his hands with the hose and then said, "You want to go turn the water off?"

Gail turned off the water faucet on the side of the house, then went and slumped miserably onto the park bench Lissa had, in an attack of whimsy, bought that month and put in the middle of the garden. She watched as Shigata neatly coiled the hose and returned it to the hook on which it normally hung.

Then Shigata went and sat down beside her, and after a moment she cuddled against him, as she used to do years ago while watching television. "You want to talk about it?" he asked.

"Uh-uh." Her voice was muffled; he thought she might be crying again.

But after a moment, her voice still muffled, she said, "When I was twelve, when that woman got killed in the alley behind our house, I saw it and I knew she was dead, but I—it never was really *real*. I didn't see her up close. I didn't know what she looked like. And I know my—my other mom—I knew she was dead. But I didn't see her. That man— I saw his face. I never saw a dead person's face before. I— Daddy, do all dead people look like that?"

"No, of course not," Shigata said. "He was strangled. That ruptures small blood vessels in the face and makes the eyes bulge, and the lack of fresh oxygenated blood to the head causes that purplish color. Most dead people, their faces look extremely relaxed. Their jaws drop a little so their mouths are open just a bit, and their faces get very pale because the blood drains away—that's assuming they're lying on their backs, of course. The blood kind of pools in the lowermost part of the body. Except for that very waxy look of the body, which is partly the paleness and partly the extreme stillness no one ever achieves in life, most dead people just look as if they're very deeply asleep with their eyes open."

"That wasn't what I meant, though," Gail said. "I mean, I know he was strangled and that made his face look weird. It was just— What I meant, he was there but it was like—like there was nobody home. Does that make sense?"

"The house is vacant and the windows stare," Shigata quoted softly.

"Yeah! Like that," Gail said. "Where'd you get that?"

"A poem Hansen wrote, years ago," Shigata said. "About the first suicide he worked. He gave it to me last month, when that fellow shot himself at the gas station, because the suicide he wrote about had been in the same place." (And Johnny Quinn, Shigata reflected uneasily, had that job now.)

"Do you remember all of it?"

"I don't know," Shigata said. "I think so. Let me give it a shot—

> *The house is vacant and the windows stare.*
> *The gray-faced corpse leans backward in the chair.*
> *His life was bounded by what claims him, dead.*
> *A rusty oil can's beside his waxen head—*
> *A shapeless black felt hat grotesquely lies*
> *Atop his head and covers up his eyes.*
> *His pocket holds the tool for checking air.*
> *His hat pulled sideways covers up his hair.*
> *His pants pull up to show white cotton socks.*
> *His death was bounded by—an ice cream box.*
> *Well, bear him hence and cover up his face.*
> *Another corpse will stand in this one's place.*
> *So yes, he died, but one more answer give:*
> *Say yes, he died, but did he ever live?"*

Gail took a deep breath. "Yeah," she said. "Like that. I wish I could memorize stuff the way you do. I have to work and work if I need to remember something, and you just look at it and it's in your head forever, it seems like."

"Which means my head's always full of unwanted flotsam and jetsam," Shigata replied, working at lightness. "I wish I didn't memorize so easily. Gail, bear in mind that death— those deaths—were suicides. A man who spent his entire life in the same dingy place, doing the same thankless job— not even a mechanic, which can be pretty interesting—but forty years of just pumping gas and checking tires, until one day he couldn't face one more hour of the boredom and put a bullet through his head. You don't have to wonder whether Ralph Miner lived. He lived. He lived his life very, very fully— much more so than most people do."

"And maybe that makes him deader than the guy at the service station was," Gail said.

"Maybe," Shigata conceded. "I hadn't thought about it that way, but yeah, maybe you're right."

Gail was silent, staring at the garden without, apparently, really seeing it. Then, abruptly, she asked, "Do you ever wish you had some kids of your own, instead of just me?"

"Gail," Shigata said, "when I adopted you, you became my own child."

"But you know what I mean."

"Okay, yes, I know what you mean. I don't know—I don't guess I've thought about it much, at least not consciously."

"Why don't you and Mom have some more kids?"

"I'm too old."

"Oh, come on," Gail said, and then blushed violently.

In the twilight, Shigata could feel his face burning also. "That's not what I mean," he said. "I mean I'm pushing fifty. If your mom and I had a baby tomorrow, which obviously we aren't going to do, I'd be around seventy—if I were still alive, which I wouldn't care to gamble on—by the time that child graduated from college. It wouldn't be fair to bring a child into the world if I had every reason to believe I wouldn't live long enough to raise it."

"Then we could—you could—adopt more kids. They're already in the world, no matter who adopts them."

"The state wouldn't let somebody my age adopt," Shigata said, "and I happen to think the state's right about that, for reasons just stated."

"Not a baby they wouldn't," Gail agreed. "But an older kid—they're always hunting parents for older kids. And if the kid was older then you'd be younger when the kid was grown up."

Shigata sighed, after working his way through the convoluted reasoning. "You don't give up, do you?"

Gail's cheeks dimpled in a smile. "No," she said smugly.

"What brought this discussion on, anyway?"

"I don't know—I guess I was just thinking. Partly about that man in the fish tank—Ralph Miner. He died and nobody cared. That creep Todd even thought it was funny."

"I doubt he really thought it was funny," Shigata said. "Remember, he saw his mother and sister after they were shot, and he's never fully gotten over that. My guess is he was acting like a jerk to cover up a real horror he couldn't admit."

"Maybe," Gail said, sounding unconvinced. "But all the same, nobody really cared that Ralph Miner was dead. I cared about seeing a body, but I didn't care that it was Ralph Miner. He didn't have a family. Todd Hansen told me that, too. He said his dad was about the only friend Mr. Miner had left, and even his dad didn't really like him anymore. And I was just thinking, families are important. Really important. And I have you and Mom, but you're my parents, and—and you're older than me. You and Mom both. And I never thought about this before, but one day you and Mom won't be there anymore and then I'll wish I had some brothers and sisters. I mean, we learn in school about ecology and zero population growth and the world is getting too full of people and all that, but when you think about it—Mom, and both her sisters, and Henry Samford, and you—all together just produced one offspring, and that's me, and that's not zero population growth, that's negative population growth. Five dwindling down to one."

"Quinn made up for us," Shigata drawled. "Two produced twelve."

"All right," Gail said. "But a kid who's already born is already born. So you wouldn't be responsible—"

"Where would we put another child?" Shigata asked, with the feeling that he was fighting a losing battle. "The house is too small as it is."

"We could add on to it. Or get a bigger house."

"I can't afford that."

"Mom can."

And that was true. Melissa Shigata, despite her efforts to get rid of it, still had over $4 million of Henry Samford's money left. As far as Shigata was concerned, Melissa deserved every penny of it, after what Samford had put her through. A reasonable argument could be made that Gail deserved at least part of it.

But Shigata? Henry Samford didn't owe him for anything, except maybe thirty cents for the bullet Shigata had killed

him with—that, and the worst week of Shigata's life. But
how do you quantify terror, agony, grief, into dollars and
cents?

"I'll think about it," Shigata said. "And talk with your
mom about it. But that's all I can promise right now. Go get
cleaned up; we're going out for dinner. I'll get the bathroom
after you."

Gail wrinkled her nose. "You better get it before me."

"Am I that bad?"

"Shave," Ed Quinn said.

"Ah, come on," Todd Hansen argued. "It's after dark, and
we're just going—"

"To work," Ed said. "Going to work at an amusement park
isn't the same as going to an amusement park to ride the
rides. We're going to work. But we're not going anywhere
until you shave."

"You didn't tell me this morning to shave, before we went
to apply for the job."

"This morning you were still okay. Now you're not. Shave."

"Anyway, we weren't scheduled to start work till tomorrow."

"For the third time I'm telling you, Hobby called my house
and said he wanted us to come in tonight."

"You didn't have to say we would."

"The man who pays the salary calls the shots," Ed said,
not very patiently. "Now hurry up and shave. We're supposed to pick up passes and identification and stuff at the
west gate by seven o'clock."

As Todd stalked off in the direction of the bathroom, Ed
looked, with some irritation, around the living room. He
could only assume that both Todd and his father had been
living on an exclusive diet of carry-out hamburgers, carry-
out Chinese food, and carry-out pizza. Well, that made a
little sense, he supposed, but was there any particular reason
why they couldn't put the hamburger wrappers, sweet and
sour pork containers, and pizza boxes into the trash?

Unable to stand and look at the mess any longer, he

grabbed one of the 7-Eleven sacks that lay around the room—apparently they had served to carry home the Coca-Cola, bottles of which were also littering the house—and began to stuff trash into it. He was filling the fifth bag when Todd returned from the bathroom and stopped short. "Hey, man, what do you think you're doing?"

"Your job," Ed snapped. "Since you're too lazy to get off your ass and do it yourself."

"Who appointed you my boss?"

"Am I my brother's keeper?" Ed proclaimed. "Well, you aren't my brother, but you damn sure need a keeper. Why don't you help me pick up some of this stuff? It won't take five minutes. Then you can leave a note so your dad'll know where you went—"

"My dad won't give a shit where I went," Todd retorted, stuffing hamburger wrappers into a Burger King bag. "He's off somewhere screwing Claire Barndt."

"Leave a note anyway," Ed said.

Steve Hansen was not in bed with Claire Barndt. He was fully clothed in the denim jeans and chambray shirt he lived in off duty, sitting in her living room, which wasn't in much better shape than his own, arguing with her—or, more precisely at the moment, listening to her argue.

"I know what I'm doing." Claire, in an aqua jogging suit that concealed just about everything, delicately scraped an anchovy off the top of a pizza and put it in her mouth.

"Why don't you eat the damn pizza like a human being?"

"I don't like the crust."

"Then why did you ask for a pizza to start with?"

"I didn't," Claire said. "I just said I'd rather have a pizza than chow mein."

"And if you had chow mein you wouldn't eat the rice."

"I don't like rice."

"Neither does Shigata."

"What's that supposed to prove?" she asked angrily.

"Not a damn thing," Hansen said. "Just, whoever heard of a Japanese not liking rice?"

"He's not Japanese. His ancestors were Japanese. Mine weren't. And you don't care what I eat anyway; you're just bitching about that because you don't know what else to bitch about."

"I know what else I want to bitch about."

"Steve," she said in a mock-patient tone, "I told you the day we met—"

"Remet—"

"Remet, then. I told you then that I didn't intend to stay in Bayport for the rest of my life. I didn't then and I don't now. I'm joining the Secret Service. I've applied, and I've taken all their tests, and I've passed all their tests, and I've had all my interviews, and I'm going—"

"You don't need to tell me again. I heard you the first time." Hansen shoved the pizza box away from him.

"I have a perfect right to—"

"I never said you didn't."

"And I never said anything was going to be permanent."

"I know you didn't," Hansen said. "Keep talking. Maybe you'll convince yourself you're right."

"I *am* right." She picked up the pizza box, looked at it moodily, and put it down again. "You could always come with me."

"Right," he said. "Like the Secret Service always hires overage ex-cons."

"You're not a—"

"I spent three years on death row, don't tell me I'm not—"

"And now you're legally exonerated, so don't tell me—"

"That doesn't make me any younger," Hansen said. "They have an age limit. I'm over it. Anyway I've got a son to raise, and I'm doing a lousy enough job of that as it is. If I had to be ready to go halfway around the world on half an hour's notice—"

"That doesn't happen very often."

"The hell it doesn't," Hansen said. "How many Secret Service agents have you talked to lately?"

"More than you have."

"Fine. Have you listened to them?"

"I listened. Look, can we discontinue this discussion?"

"Fine," Hansen answered. "Consider it discontinued." He stood up and reached for his car keys.

"Where are you going?"

"Out to check on my son. You know, that kid who lives with me? Todd? After that, I don't know. Probably back out to ArkPark."

"How come?"

"What do you mean how come? Because there's a series of murders going on there, that's how come." He headed for the front door and paused by the telephone stand. "And quit taking your phone off the hook. I guarantee the Secret Service won't let you do it. You're supposed to be on twenty-four-hour call here, but when *they* say twenty-four-hour call, they mean it." He slammed the receiver back down onto the hook.

"Yes, sir, sergeant, sir," Claire called after him, as he headed out the door.

"I can't help it." The dispatcher sounded harassed. "Captain Quinn's already left for ArkPark on that surveillance thing he was supposed to go on later tonight, so—"

"What did he do that for?" Shigata interrupted. "He wasn't due out there for hours. I told him to go get some sleep."

"I don't know why he went out there early. He said something about carrots and hippopotamuses or something like that. You know how he gets when he's thinking. But anyhow he's out there and so he can't be sent out on something else, and I can't find Sergeant Hansen. He was at Corporal Barndt's house, but he left and apparently he's not home yet, or at least he's not answering his telephone. So I haven't got anybody else to call."

"Okay, okay, I'm on my way," Shigata said wearily. To Lissa, he added, "That's the problem with having only three investigators and one of them's me."

"What have you got?"

"Armed robbery, that Seven-Eleven right off I-45. Like

there's something I can do about it—whoever did it is probably halfway to Houston or Galveston by now. I don't know how late I'll be. Why don't you and Gail go on out and get something to eat?"

"We'll wait for you," Lissa said.

"Suit yourself. If that photographer calls—his name is Chester Stratford—tell him I'll call him back."

The robber was a Hispanic male, about five-eight, a hundred and thirty pounds, black hair, brown eyes. He'd been wearing blue jeans, a denim jacket, and a Bart Simpson T-shirt. He'd had a small black pistol, caliber anything from .22 to .38, make anything from RG to Colt or Smith & Wesson. There wouldn't be any use sending for a police artist or somebody with a composite kit, because he'd been wearing a pair of panty hose over his head, which had thoroughly masked his features. He'd left in a blue car that might be a Lynx or an Escort or something like that; the "something like that," Shigata reflected, effectively took in approximately half the automobiles on the road. There was no use dusting for fingerprints, because he hadn't touched anything in the store, including the door, which he'd opened with his shoulder (which suggested he might have been caught on fingerprints once before, and that was the only even vaguely possible lead). He'd gotten only about twenty-five dollars, because the clerk—a young woman—was careful about putting money into the safe when she was supposed to.

Outside, Shigata said to Corporal Ted Barlow, who was shift supervisor at the moment, "Please try to avoid calling me out unless it looks as if there's really something I can do."

"I wouldn't have called you this time," Barlow answered calmly, "except I know her. And I know her boyfriend. And he's a television newsman."

After a moment, Shigata said, "Oh."

"Chester Stratford called while you were out," Lissa said. "He told me to tell you that if you were calling him about that video camera that was submerged in the aquarium at

ArkPark, the sooner he could get to it the more likely it'd be that he'd be able to salvage it. So I told him you'd bring it down to him tonight if you got home in time. He said he'll be up until about midnight. Here's his address."

Shigata accepted the index card with the Galveston address written on it. "We might as well drop it by and then get something to eat," he said. "I'd had in mind driving up toward Houston, but I guess Galveston's just as good."

And it might have been, until he parked in front of a seafood restaurant ten minutes after delivering the videotape and Gail said, "Yuck. I'm not going in there."

"Why not?" Shigata asked.

"Really, Mark!" Lissa protested. "You ought to realize—"

"I'm never going to eat fish again," Gail said. "Never in my whole life. The fishes were nibbling at that man's face. I didn't know fishes ate people. I don't want any supper anyway. Let's just go home." She lay down in the backseat.

"Seat belt, Gail," Shigata said.

"I'm wearing two seat belts," she said without moving. "One around my knees and one around my shoulders."

Shigata was tempted to let her stay there. But if the car happened to be rammed from the side, her head would be the first thing hit. "Sit up and put your seat belt on right," he said. "We'll stop at McDonald's and get some hamburgers on the way home."

"If we knew what we were supposed to be doing," Todd said crossly, "I'll bet we could do it better."

"You're probably right," Ed returned. "But since we don't, just keep walking and looking for anything that looks funny, like Mr. Hobby said to do."

"We've been walking for two hours."

"Good. Now we get to walk some more."

"We could stop and eat."

"You got any money?"

"No," Todd said. "Don't you?"

"Surely you jest. If I could get money without having a job I wouldn't need a job, now would I?"

"Anyway how're we supposed to know what looks funny?" Todd demanded. "We've only been here once before."

"Danged if I know," Ed said. He paused, listening to the discord of rams' horns followed by the low, sustained rumble that told him the walls of Jericho had tumbled down for the tenth time that day.

"I never thought I could get tired of a theme park," Todd complained.

"You're going to get a lot tireder of this one before the summer's over." Ed stopped short. "Have a look over there."

"What am I supposed to be looking at?"

"I don't know. Over there. How does that look to you?"

"I didn't know there was a door there," Todd said slowly.

"Neither did I. So maybe we ought to have a look."

▽

Chapter 7

ONCE WHEN QUINN WAS still working oil field security, he'd had to go to the Galveston Police Department for something. He couldn't even remember now what it was, except that it had involved a whole lot of waiting, mostly in the detective bureau. While there, he'd watched an experienced detective—watched him because he was really puzzled about what the man was doing.

The detective was sitting at his desk, completely silently, holding in both hands a heavy plastic sleeve containing a forged check. He just sat there, looking at the check, for over two hours. Then, with a broad grin, he stood up, grabbed a hand radio and a set of car keys, and went out the door. He was back twenty minutes later with a young man in handcuffs. The young man denied the forgery for about twenty minutes; then, as suddenly as the detective had gone out the door, he grinned and said, "Well, I guess you got me again, didn't you? I sure do wish I knew how you do that."

Then Quinn, still in his twenties and fairly new to law enforcement, had found it totally impossible to imagine how two hours of staring at a forged check had suddenly produced a suspect. Now, he came a lot closer to understanding.

Because there are some police who work strictly by the rules, paint by the numbers, so to speak—and Hansen,

Quinn knew now, no matter how brilliant he was, would never be much more than a by-the-rules cop, because his people sense was sadly deficient. There are police who combine paint-by-number policing with hunch and instinct, and they are probably the best cops around. Shigata, Quinn had pretty well decided, would fit into that category most of the time, although occasionally he was far more rule driven than Quinn really liked. And there are some police who fly almost entirely by the seats of their pants; they act on instinct or conditioned reflex; and those cops can sometimes make pretty amazing leaps in reasoning. Quinn figured that was the category he—and that detective in Galveston so long ago—belonged in.

But this time Quinn and that instinct, that conditioned reflex, weren't getting along so well. His subconscious was trying to tell him something, and he couldn't figure out what it was, except that it was certainly connected to ArkPark. So at the moment all he could think of to do was wander aimlessly around the park, observing everything he could observe.

Observing was not the easiest job in the world just now. For one thing, it was pitch dark, and the bright lights created a multitude of dark shadows that could hide an army of criminals. On top of that, either Bayport was not the only school in the area to have had a teacher workday or else as soon as school had gotten out for the weekend every kid in Southeast Texas had headed for ArkPark. Quinn estimated that there were 12,000 to 15,000 people there right now, at least 10,000 to 13,000 of them under twenty, and at least 2,000 of them standing in line for the chance to sling stones at Goliath, who looked distinctly like an enlarged rubber or plastic Saddam Hussein. Another 500 or so were waiting for the chance to pay money to write graffiti on the walls of Jericho before they fell down again (and then rerose minus graffiti, and how in the world did they do *that*?). He wondered whether the city council had stopped to think, when it had approved the building of ArkPark inside the city limits, that when it was running at full capacity—when most of the area schools were closed—the park would more than double the population of the city.

He couldn't help noticing—and at times finding it almost as funny as Hansen did, though in a different sort of way—how Hobby had struggled to carry out the idea of the Ark in setting up his zoo. He'd obviously struggled valiantly to figure out what animals were ritually clean according to Genesis, and therefore should be collected in sevens, and what animals were ritually unclean, and therefore to be collected only in twos. What, he wondered, did he intend to do with the offspring of the twos and the sevens? Keep them, as he probably assumed Noah had done (unless he'd decided to assume that the animals on the Ark had temporarily ceased reproducing), or sell them to a zoo? But that wasn't likely to be possible; most zoos around the world were suffering financial problems, and many of them were more likely to be selling animals from their collections than buying more animals or even accepting donations. Whatever Hobby was going to do, he'd better decide fast, because he was soon to have fifty-odd baby alligators besides the two (alligators being unclean animals) he'd started out with—and alligators, oddly enough, tend to be very protective parents.

ArkPark tried to carry out the theme of the Bible in more than the zoo. Quinn stopped at a food kiosk for a dish of manna—which looked to him very much like vanilla ice cream, at an inflated price—and rejected the locust topping (your choice of mint chocolate or plain chocolate). Soft drinks, he noticed, were offered by the firkin, which seemed to have shrunk from its original meaning of about nine gallons down to twenty ounces. He wondered what in the world ArkPark would call hamburgers, hot dogs, or pizza but decided he wasn't curious enough to walk over to the hot food booths to find out. He couldn't, however, help noticing the large sign offering Sea of Galilee Fish and Chips.

Once again he let himself wonder how in the world Hobby had managed to come up with the money to build ArkPark, which combined a zoo—a really good zoo, all things considered—with a moderately varied theme park. He couldn't imagine how much it would cost to set up a place like this—probably under a billion dollars, but certainly millions, probably tens of millions, maybe even hundreds of millions. Well, maybe that was an overestimate. But, besides setting it up, Hobby had to run it, and that included a staff—probably a fairly large staff, even if he did also make use of the residents of his homeless shelter—as well as food and water for a lot of animals, some of whom would eat carrots and hay but some of whom would certainly want meat. A lot of meat.

Hobby's television ministry had been on the air only six months. It couldn't have raised that kind of money that fast—especially not in view of the fact that ArkPark had already been well under construction, in fact almost finished, by the time the television show had started.

While Quinn had been thinking the crowd had thinned out, and lights were going off, gradually, around the park. He'd need to head over to the office building soon, but for the moment he stopped, one foot on a railing, to look down pensively at the seals frolicking in their share of the pool where Ralph Miner had died. Only two seals; apparently Hobby had decided seals were unclean animals. Quinn wondered whether that was correct.

One sure thing: Whether seals are clean or unclean, they eat fish, not carrots. Especially not forty pounds of carrots.

Rabbits eat carrots, but it would take an awful lot of rabbits to eat forty pounds' worth. Anyway, if you want to move a rabbit, you don't have to lure it out of the way. If it doesn't move when you approach it—which probably it will—all you have to do is pick it up and move it.

Zebras would eat carrots. Antelopes probably would. But again, you don't have to lure them out of the way. If you want to be where the zebra or antelope is, you head that way and the zebra or antelope will move. They don't trust humans. They're probably smart that way.

Will rhinos eat carrots? Quinn hadn't the slightest idea. He did know they're stupid and almost blind, and they function by sense of smell, though it's hard to imagine how they smell anything other than themselves. Also they're extremely unpredictable, so that if you offered a carrot to a rhino it might take the carrot but it might gore you before— or after—taking it.

For some reason he couldn't fathom, except that maybe it was a hunch his conscious mind couldn't explain, he kept thinking about hippos. He hadn't the slightest idea whether hippos are clean or unclean animals; he did know ArkPark had only one, rather than two or seven, probably because one was all they could afford or locate.

He could, of course, be wrong in the whole idea that the purpose of the carrots was to lure an animal into, or out of, a particular spot. But he didn't think he was wrong. He strolled over to have a quick look at the hippo, before going to the office and sitting down to spend the night looking at television monitors.

Someone called to him, and he turned to see who it was.

Hansen was technically off duty. But Todd had taken off (to work, as unlikely as that seemed), and Claire Barndt apparently was now history, at least as far as Hansen was concerned. His choices were to read, to watch television, to go to a movie, or to go back to work. Because he had too much adrenaline built up to sit still, that seemed to narrow it down to going back to work.

To him, the whole case seemed to structure itself as a delicate balancing act, and if he could just find a way to bring it off balance—to find the center of balance and tinker with it a little—he'd know exactly, or almost exactly, what was going on.

He didn't think Ralph Miner was the center of balance. Miner had spent his entire life being in exactly the wrong place at exactly the wrong time, usually meddling in other people's business, and almost certainly he'd ended his life doing exactly that. So who was the center of balance? Ruskin? Maybe, but he doubted it; he suspected that she, like Miner, had simply managed to carry her curiosity too far. Hobby? Maybe—but that, too, he was beginning to doubt. Someone around Hobby? Perhaps, but who?

Was the balance a what, instead of a who? If so, it was certainly ArkPark. But that still posed a problem. Ralph Miner would hang around ArkPark without any encouragement, but the chances of Margaret Ruskin deciding out of the blue to go to ArkPark were exactly zero. That meant either that someone had brought her body to ArkPark, which seemed senseless, or that something had caused her to decide to go to ArkPark, and that something had almost certainly developed as a direct result of her meddling. Of that, Hansen felt certain, because, if it had developed out of her membership on the city council, there would have been something in council records to tip him off.

So where did she meddle most? Her rental houses, obviously.

Quinn had already talked to people there. So had Shigata. Now Hansen intended to make a visit.

Shigata had started out at the Athanasopoulous house. Quinn, of course, had started with Johnny Quinn. Hansen decided to start with Lynette Evans.

She was, as Johnny Quinn had said, black. She was about thirty-five, very pretty, very neat, and seemingly well organized. The oldest daughter, Jean, was in the kitchen washing the dishes; the other two girls, Mary and Connie, were sitting at the table doing homework. Evans was sewing, and as she answered Hansen's questions she went on making hand-stitched buttonholes in a pink blouse the right size for Connie.

"It was easy to get mad at Mrs. Ruskin," she said carefully, "but I tried to remind myself she really wanted to be helpful. I know what Mrs. A said, about her coming over here and showing her the house, but I don't think she thought for a minute how thoughtless and spiteful it seemed. She was just trying to get it across that she cared about her property and wanted other people to care about it too. I remember one time when I was sick she came over and mowed the lawn for me—didn't stop to realize, of course, that when I was in bed with flu I didn't exactly *want* to hear a lawn mower running right outside my bedroom window. And part of the reason she was mad about the house being such a mess was that I wouldn't let her clean it up."

"Let her clean it up?" Hansen repeated, somewhat startled.

Evans nodded. "She has this thing about helping people. If you don't have time to clean your house, she'll come and help you—invited or uninvited. I came home one time to find her washing my breakfast dishes, and I told her not to come back in uninvited. Besides that, another reason she was mad at me was, I caught her in a dumb mistake once."

Hansen waited.

"It was when the house the A's have now was vacant. I should mention that Mrs. Ruskin's idea of clean and everybody else's idea of clean don't always jibe. The people who moved out, their name was Greenwood or Greentree or something like that, had actually left the place pretty clean. I know because I helped them move. But Mrs. Ruskin decided the toilet wasn't clean enough, and she tried to clean it by mixing toilet bowl cleaner and chlorine bleach. Now, everybody knows not to do that, or ought to know anyway—it says on the bleach container and the toilet bowl cleaner both. But she did. Fortunately she'd opened the bathroom window first, and when I parked my car—my parking place is between my house and that one—I heard her coughing. By the time I could get into the house, she was semi-conscious and I had to drag her out into the hall and then call an ambulance. She was really mad at me for that. She said she'd have been okay without the ambulance. Well, maybe she would, but I didn't want to risk it."

All this, Hansen thought, was interesting in terms of what it told him about Margaret Ruskin's personality. But he couldn't see that it told him anything at all about who killed her.

Evans was still talking. "Mrs. A was just furious at her one time—you know they've got that boy, Junior they call him. He's nineteen or so, and you know how teenagers keep their rooms, and one day Mrs. A came home and Mrs. Ruskin was in there cleaning Junior's room. Well, Junior's not a bad kid, he didn't have dope or anything like that in there, but he did have a couple of *Playboy*s or something like that, and the way Mrs. Ruskin carried on—well!"

And Junior works at ArkPark . . . the first possible link, Hansen thought. What else did she find in Junior's room, besides the girlie magazines? "How long ago was this?" he asked.

"Oh, heavens, I don't know, two or three months. Well, it couldn't be that long, they just moved in two months ago. Why don't you ask Mrs. A? As mad as she was, she'll probably remember. Is there anything else you'd like me to tell you? I know I've just been chattering, but—"

"You've been a lot of help," Hansen said. "So often it's the personality of the victim that determines the crime. The more we know about the victim, the better off we are. Now, if you don't mind, I'll drop on over and talk with Mrs. A."

"I think she's left for work," Evans said. "But maybe not."

She hadn't. Normally she would have, she said, but she'd taken the day off.

"I don't see why people have trouble with your name," Hansen told her. "Athanasopoulous has a lot of syllables, but they're easy syllables."

Mrs. Athanasopoulous laughed. "You may not have trouble with it, but I do. My maiden name was Papogouras. Now, that's an easy name. I kid you not, I honestly thought about refusing to marry George just so I wouldn't have to have a name I can hardly pronounce—or spell, for that matter. So I'd really rather you just call me Irene. Or Mrs. A, if you'd rather."

"Irene's fine. And my name's Steve, if you don't mind calling a cop by his first name."

She shrugged. "Don't make me no nevermind. Cops, deputy sheriffs, they come into the restaurant a lot at night. Firemen don't—they eat at the fire station. So I don't get to know firemen. No offense, but how come you're here? I mean, I've already talked with two cops."

"No offense taken," he said. "I just—I'm hardheaded, I guess. I always want to go ask my own questions even if I know other people have asked. Maybe I'm just nosy."

Irene laughed. "Maybe you are. Lord knows she was. Mrs. Ruskin, I mean."

"Yeah, Mrs. Evans told me about her trying to clean your son's room."

"She didn't just *try* to do it, she *did* do it," Irene said. "One thing about it, Junior sure has kept his room cleaner since then—I guess he's afraid she'll come back and clean it again if he doesn't."

"How long ago did that happen?" Hansen asked, as casually as possible.

"Oh, Lord, I don't know, right after we moved in, probably two months ago. Way before the park opened—Junior was still working real irregular hours, helping to get it ready to open up."

Hansen asked a few more questions he didn't really want to know the answers to, because he wanted to get away and think without making it too clear what he was thinking about.

Junior Athanasopoulous, at the moment, was the only visible link between Margaret Ruskin and ArkPark. But was he the only link? Was it conceivable that Ruskin had found something—say, the ivory—in his room, and kept it quiet this long?

Maybe there was another connection.

Maybe Johnny Quinn would know. Maybe nobody had thought of the right way to ask him.

Maybe Pablo Gonzales and his wife, Joyce, would know. Nobody had talked with them yet.

But Hansen, feeling now the aftermath of his anger as he'd left Claire's apartment, didn't have any huge desire to go talk with them himself.

He sat for a moment in his car, put the key in the ignition, and briefly turned his head to the left. There was a light on in the Ruskin house, and somebody moved past a window.

Quite suddenly, the adrenaline was pumping again, and Hansen was silently cursing himself for having been fool enough to take off on any phase of an investigation without having a radio along. He got out of the car and walked over to the Quinn house, which was closest except for the Gonzales apartment, which was upstairs, and the Gonzaleses didn't know him anyway.

When Johnny came to the door, Hansen said, "I need your phone, fast."

Johnny stepped back and pointed. "It's over there."

Cursing every second it took to dial, Hansen dialed the police station and said, "Get me a backup in front of Margaret Ruskin's house on Crockett. I've got prowlers inside the house. Run silent, no siren or anything. Tell him when he gets there, tap his horn twice to let me know he's in place. Then I'm going in from the back."

"Ten-four," the dispatcher said.

Hansen hung up, and Johnny said, "You need any help?"

"I can't ask a civilian for help on something like this."

Johnny grinned. "Guess what? I was sworn in as a Galveston County deputy sheriff at two o'clock this afternoon."

"Then get ready and let's go."

Johnny headed for the hall, returning seconds later wearing a gun belt that, from its age, was clearly an Al Quinn hand-me-down. But never mind that, the gun in its holster was clean and loaded, and Hansen had no doubt whatever that Johnny knew how to use it, besides having—as all the Quinn kids had—a goodly share of plain old horse sense.

It felt like hours; in fact it could not have been more than five minutes before a car horn honked, briefly, twice, from Crockett Street. Hansen and Johnny moved as quietly as possible in the darkness toward the back door, which was, of course, locked . . . and without a no-knock warrant they'd be on risky grounds breaking it down even if they did have prowlers in the house. Hansen stood, frustrated, and Johnny quite simply reached out and rang the doorbell. Which was, come to think of it, exactly what Quinn would have done given the same situation.

After a moment, a male voice from inside the house called, "Who is it?"

"Police," Hansen answered. "Open up."

"On my way." Shortly, a bolt slid back and the door opened.

They had two prowlers, not one. One was about five-eight, dark brown hair, brown eyes, bearing such a very distinct resemblance to a masculinized Margaret Ruskin that Hansen felt fairly safe in saying, "Are you Calvin Ruskin?"

"Yeah. Who are you at this time of night?"

"Sergeant Steve Hansen, Bayport Police Department. This is Deputy Johnny Quinn of the Galveston County Sheriff's Department." Hansen produced identification; Johnny did not. "We thought you were prowlers."

"Well, as you can see, we're not. So if you'll let us get on about our business—"

"Actually we can't see you're not," Johnny said, perfectly amiably. "You said you're Calvin Ruskin, but we haven't seen any identification, and you haven't said a word about your companion there."

Hansen felt a brief annoyance. He was a veteran with over twenty years of police work; he had an IQ of 150 and a Ph.D. But it seemed that Johnny Quinn, high school graduate, with less than one day of police experience and not even born when Hansen had started policing, had better police instincts.

On the other hand, he was Al Quinn's son. Maybe there *was* something in heredity . . .

While Hansen was thinking that, Ruskin was producing his driver's license. So was the other man, who was just over six feet, with light brown hair in a military cut, light blue eyes, and a deep tan, and who turned out to be Second Lieutenant Dennis Conner.

"I see you got back," Hansen remarked. "How was Saudi?"

"Hotter'n hell," Conner replied.

"How's your wife doing?"

"She's doing fine," Conner said. "I took her home and told her to stay there and let me take care of things down here. Now can we cut the small talk? We're busy."

"I can see that," Hansen said, determined not to let Johnny take the lead again. "Looking for something?" From what little he could see through the half-open door, it was evident that a search, possibly even more thorough than the two already conducted, was in progress.

"Calvin, they're cops," Conner said. "You might as well let them in and explain. After all, there's just a chance that it might help them."

"If they haven't already found it," Ruskin replied.

"I told you you should have stopped by the police station before we started searching, just in case."

"Right," Ruskin said. "And just who do you expect to find in the Bayport Police Station at seven P.M.? One desk officer, corporal at most, more likely a patrolman, or even more likely a civilian dispatcher acting as desk officer as well. I've tried to get the police to do stuff at night in this town before. It can't be done."

"I suspect," Hansen said, working at keeping his temper, "that you tried to get the police to do stuff in this town at night when Dale Shipp was chief."

"What difference does it make who's chief?"

"A lot of difference," Hansen said, "when the chief is a former FBI agent with a J.D. degree."

"Yeah?" Ruskin said, sounding a little more interested.

"I policed under Dale Shipp," Hansen added, "and let me tell you, he wouldn't *let* his officers do anything much. Shigata's different. We're working this case hard. And if you know anything that might help us, well, we'd appreciate it if you'd let us in on it."

Ruskin and Conner looked at each other; an unspoken dialogue took place, and then Ruskin stepped back from the door and said, "Come in."

Moments later, sitting at the kitchen table with coffee, which Johnny had politely, and without explanation, declined, Ruskin said, "How much do you know about Mother and her—uh—investigations?"

"I've been told she was extremely inquisitive," Hansen said.

Conner grinned, and Ruskin barked a short fragment of laughter. "She was damn nosy, was what she was, and that's what you were told. Okay, it was true. Part of it was nothing in the world but curiosity; it drove her nuts anytime there was something going on and she didn't know all about it.

She wasn't mean-spirited about it; she didn't use what she found out to hurt people, at least not deliberately; she just plain wanted to know. But part of it—" He toyed with the handle of the coffee mug, choosing his words now with considerable care.

"Part of it, I think, was that she sort of thought of her position as a city councilor as meaning somewhat more than it did. She'd have made a good investigative reporter. She'd have made a good cop. She ferreted things out. She didn't try to turn anything she found out over to the Bayport police; I suppose she must have been aware of the change in chief, but apparently she didn't figure it meant much. She turned stuff over to the Galveston County District Attorney's Office, or even a few times to the state attorney general."

"I'm astonished I never heard anything about this," Hansen said.

Ruskin smiled slightly. "You weren't meant to. She tried to make very sure nobody in the Bayport Police Department ever heard about it."

Thinking about Shipp, Hansen said, "Up until three years ago, she'd have been right. But since then—"

"It probably killed her," Conner said roughly. He'd been sitting, silently, listening. "We both told her to lay off; she didn't know what she was getting into, she didn't have any kind of safety network, it was dangerous; but she never would listen. She never even told Amy about it."

"Did Moira know?" Hansen asked.

Conner grimaced. "Are you kidding? Moira would have tried to call up the ghost of Captain Galvez to help with the investigation—whatever the investigation was. Get on with it, Calvin. Tell them what she was up to this time."

Ruskin looked down at the table, eyes blank, as if he weren't really seeing it at all. "She told me," he said in a low voice, "that she had some information about smuggling. She said this was really big, the biggest thing she'd ever found out. I told her if it was, then it was also the riskiest, and she'd better lay off. Call the feds in, if it was real smuggling. She got mad at me. She told me she could investigate it a lot easier than they could and a lot more efficiently. She was keeping a journal of what she'd found out and how she'd found it, and when she was ready she'd turn it and the other evidence she'd collected over to the Border Patrol and the FBI. She told me she was hiding the journal where nobody would ever find it. Well—we were trying to find it. That's all."

Then, violently, he added, "I don't want her to have died for nothing. Doesn't that make sense? To want to know what she died for? To want to lay my hands on that information, and use it?"

"Of course it makes sense," Hansen said. "But you're not the only one who wanted to lay hands on that information."

"What do you mean?"

"Mr. Conner, all your mother's keys are missing. And when Chief Shigata and Captain Quinn got here to start their own search for evidence, they found the house had already been searched, very thoroughly."

Ruskin slammed his fist down on the table. "Shit!" he yelled.

"You should have guessed," Conner said placidly. "*We* should have guessed. If they killed her, they knew she was onto something. Of course they wanted to find anything she might have written down."

"That doesn't mean there's no use at all in your looking too," Hansen said. "We didn't know we were looking for a journal. There's a good chance they didn't either. Which means there's at least a halfway chance you might find it. Meanwhile, is there anything else at all she said that might help us figure out what she was looking for, or at? Maybe why she wound up at ArkPark?"

"She said part of what was happening was happening at ArkPark. She said you had to go there in the middle of the night to tell anything about it. I told her she was absolutely crazy—if she thought a big smuggling ring was using Ark-Park, the last thing in the world she or anybody else unarmed needed to be doing was running around ArkPark in the middle of the night. She told me to mind my own business. She'd found a safe place to sneak in at night, so nobody would ever spot her. She'd gotten a guy with a video camera to help her. She said he was really strange, but he was just as interested as she was in what was going on."

Hansen, suddenly feeling his heart pounding, asked, "Do you know what his name was? The guy with the video camera?"

Ruskin and Conner looked at each other. Then Ruskin said, "No. She probably told me, but I didn't have any reason to remember. Seems to me it was like the name of a job. It was a person's name, but it sounded like a job."

"Carpenter? Butcher? Miner?" Hansen tried to sound as if he were throwing out names at random.

Ruskin snapped his fingers. "Miner! That's it. Why? You think he might have been involved—?"

"No," Hansen said. "No, Ralph Miner wasn't involved. He was a friend of mine. And he's dead too." He stood up. "I appreciate your help. And the coffee. If you find the journal, here's Chief Shigata's telephone number. Call him anytime, day or night. And go to see him tomorrow. He's got something he'll want you to look at. In the meantime I'm going to just—go see what I can find at ArkPark in the middle of the night."

"Dad's already out there," Johnny said, standing also.

"I know," Hansen said. "But he's supposed to be monitoring those television screens. And it stands to reason, if there's something they don't want him to see, it won't be on the television screens while he's in there."

"Makes sense," Johnny said. "You want me to go out there with you?"

"No, thanks. I'll be okay. I'll stop by the office and write Shigata a note, tell him what's going on. I won't be out there long—I'll just have a quick look around, and then go home and get some sleep."

"Good luck," Johnny said amiably and headed back in the direction of his house.

Unlike Margaret Ruskin, Hansen didn't try to sneak into ArkPark. He found a security guard and flashed his badge, and the guard—well aware that there'd already been two murders at night in the park—made no objections to letting him in.

And he wasn't stupid. This time, he'd picked up a radio before he left the station.

He went to the office first, to look for Quinn. Maybe taking Quinn with him when he went to prowl around the grounds would be a good idea. But Burton Wells, who was sprawled comfortably in front of the monitor bank with his feet on his desk, said, "Al Quinn? Sorry, I haven't seen him. Glenn told me before he left that Quinn was supposed to get here sometime after ten o'clock, but he's not here yet."

Hansen glanced at his watch. Eleven thirty. Most likely Quinn was still prowling around the grounds, planning to get to the office a little later. "Thanks," he said. "I'll check back in with you later, if I don't find him."

"You do that," Wells said, his attention already back on the monitors.

The crowds were gone now; the lights, though not all extinguished, were farther apart, interspersed with darkened bulbs and lamps. Not knowing what he was looking for, Hansen strolled aimlessly, just looking, as Quinn had done earlier.

About midnight, he paused. "I'll be damned," he said aloud. "I didn't realize that was a door."

He headed for it.

▽

Chapter 8

SHIGATA WAS AT HIS desk by 7:00 A.M. on Saturday, very much hoping not to get another call from ArkPark about another corpse. He read the note from Hansen with considerable interest; Hansen was able to write clearly and concisely, and what he said made sense—a lot of sense, in view of what had been going on.

But what to do with the information? If, as Margaret Ruskin apparently had at least hinted to her son and son-in-law, what was going on was well concealed, then gathering up a task force and going in with a show of strength would be a very bad idea. They might never find out what Ruskin had been looking at—or for.

No, he'd wait until Quinn and Hansen got in—which might be late, considering that Quinn had worked all night and Hansen had, at least, worked quite late—and see what either of them might have gotten last night at ArkPark, and make decisions then.

He was still waiting at eight thirty, feeling mildly annoyed but reminding himself that they, like him, needed rest, when the dispatcher announced the arrival of Dennis Conner and Calvin Ruskin.

Thanks to Hansen's note, Shigata knew who they were. Rather than just let the dispatcher send them back, he went to the front of the police station to usher them in. But it was not until they were seated in his office, at the back of the small muster room, that he asked, "Were you able to find the journal?"

"No," Ruskin said. "I see that officer—Hansen, was that his name?—did report to you."

"Yes, he did. Do you think there's anything we can do to help find it?"

"No. We think it's gone," Conner said. "But Hansen said you had found something that could be evidence. We'd like to see it."

"No problem," Shigata said and turned his chair. By now he'd put the ivory in the safe, which was directly behind his normal seat. Moments later, he laid it out on the desk, all properly labeled—the ivory from Margaret Ruskin's purse, the ivory from Margaret Ruskin's toilet tank. "Have either of you ever seen any of this before?"

He expected the usual chorus of "No," and that was what he got from Ruskin. But Conner, surprisingly, said, "Yes. I couldn't tell you for sure which of those packages it was, but she showed me an ivory bracelet and ivory hairpins about a month ago, when I was home on leave, and asked me if I thought Amy would like them for a Christmas present. She had this—kind of funny look on her face. I told her Amy probably wouldn't like them much, because that's not the kind of thing Amy wears. The truth is that if anybody tried to give Amy ivory, she'd probably throw up. She says ivory belongs on elephants."

"Did Mrs. Ruskin tell you where she got it?"

"Said something about a store in the mall—I didn't ask which mall, and she didn't say."

That wasn't too helpful, at first glance. There were three malls within an hour's drive of Bayport, probably twelve more within two or two and a half hours' drive, and Shigata didn't have the manpower to check all those malls for possibly contraband ivory, at least not very quickly. Even if he found it, there wasn't much he could do about it—not one of those malls was inside his jurisdiction.

"Kind of puzzles me, though," Conner added thoughtfully.

"What does?"

"Why she'd think about it for Amy. She *knows*—knew—
Amy hates ivory. And she never did like it much herself."

He'd picked Conner's and Ruskin's minds all he could.
There simply wasn't anything there that was of any use.
What little they knew, they'd told him this morning or Han-
sen last night. And speaking of Hansen, he really ought to
be in by now no matter how late he'd worked last night.
Shigata was reaching for the telephone when it rang.

Nguyen—as usual, her English somewhat more mangled
over the telephone than in person. "I need speak to Al."

"He's not here."

"Get on radio and tell him call me."

"Hold on." Shigata took his radio out of its charger and
keyed it. "Car One to Car Two." No answer. He tried again.
"Car One to Car Two." He returned to the phone. "I can't
raise him on the radio. When did he leave home?"

"He not home sin' yesterday morning. He call me in the
afternoon, say he work all night, come home in the morning,
but no come."

"I'll find him," Shigata promised. "I'll call you back—or
have him call you."

"Tell Ed call me too."

"Ed's not home either?" Shigata demanded, feeling somewhat more shaken.

"Ed not home either. Left last night, gonna go get that
Todd and go to work. Didn' come home. I think maybe Al
with him."

"You may be right," Shigata said slowly. "You may very
well be right. I'll get onto it and let you know when I know
something."

"Okay." She hung up promptly.

The next number Shigata dialed was that of Hansen. The
phone rang twelve times with no answer. It would be nice to
be able to assure himself that Todd and Hansen were there,

that Todd was just too lazy—as usual—to get up and answer the phone, that Hansen was still asleep because he'd worked too late last night. But Shigata couldn't make himself believe that.

Claire Barndt. This number he had to look up, but it was answered promptly, on the second ring. "Claire?"

"Yeah." A yawn. "Did I forget something?"

"I don't know," he said, confused. "Why?"

"You called me," she pointed out. "I just left. I had morning watch."

"No—I just wanted to know if you knew where Hansen was."

Another yawn. "Uh-uh. Last time I saw him was about six thirty last night. We sort of, uh, we sort of had a fight."

"You didn't hear him on the radio at all last night?" Shigata did not want to delve that deeply into his officers' personal lives.

"Uh-uh. Was he supposed to be on?"

"Possibly . . . go get some rest. I may need to call the whole department in later."

She was suddenly alert. "What's wrong?"

"I don't know yet. Go get some rest."

"Like I'm going to be able to, with you not telling me what's wrong."

"Do it anyway." Shigata hung up, meditated a moment, and dialed the number for the Metro Intelligence Unit. But before the telephone had time to ring once, he hung up again. Would they believe him?

The whole thing sounded so unlikely.

They'd believe him about two murders at ArkPark, because that much had been on television. They'd believe that ivory was—or at least might be—somehow involved, because he could show them the ivory. They might—probably would—believe he had two missing cops, and two missing teenagers who were sons of the two missing cops. They'd be somewhat less likely to believe smuggling was going on through ArkPark, on the totally unsupported word of what a dead woman had told her son and son-in-law. But when he got on to talking about forty pounds of carrots and a hippopotamus, they might begin to develop a slight tendency to telephone for what he'd heard Quinn refer to as the little men with the white coats and butterfly nets. At the very least, they would assure him he could not get a search warrant on that basis.

Which meant he didn't intend to ask for a search warrant. He was going to claim, if the question came up, that he didn't figure he needed a warrant to search public areas of the park, and that was all he was doing yet. If he actually asked for a warrant and didn't get one, then that argument would automatically become invalid.

But how intelligent would it be for him to head off to ArkPark by himself, considering the situation?

His immediate instinct was to call Quinn, because Quinn had been at his side in every major move he had made in the last three years. But he couldn't call Quinn, because Quinn was the one missing. One of the ones missing. Other than Shigata, there wasn't a person on the Bayport Police Department with a rank higher than corporal who wasn't at the moment missing.

Claire Barndt would come out, but she'd be asleep on her feet, because she'd worked midnight to 8:00 A.M. Ted Barlow would come out, but he had to work the evening watch, 4:00 P.M. till midnight.

There was Johnny Quinn, who was no longer on Shigata's conscience because he now had a job in law enforcement. He also was not on Shigata's payroll. He wasn't trained yet, and he might be working. But all the same—

Shigata reached for the phone again.

It was a motley task force indeed. A very attractive blond woman with short tousled hair and what might have been referred to as bedroom eyes; a short chunky Eurasian; and Ted Barlow, who was the only one a total stranger might possibly pick out of the group as a cop.

Shigata looked at Barlow first. "You stay here," he said. "Somebody's got to be available to ride herd on the rest of the department, and you're elected. While you're here, go through the area phone books—they're in this shelf beside my desk—and call every gift store, jewelry store, boutique, and so forth in every mall in the area. You're—" He paused, meditated briefly. "You're a stockbroker and you want to buy some ivory jewelry for your girlfriend. She doesn't want antique ivory; she just wants new ivory."

"Okay," Barlow said promptly.

"If any of them say they have it, make a big fuss about provenance. Where did it come from? Is it legal? Stockbrokers have to be bonded and you can't afford any trouble. I want to know the names of anybody that's selling ivory, but especially if they get antsy about provenance."

"Gotcha," Barlow said. He turned to reach for telephone books.

"When we get to ArkPark, we're staying together," Shigata said to the others. "That's the first thing I want to make clear. I know we could cover more ground if we fanned out, but to the best of my knowledge both Quinn and Hansen were alone when they went missing. Ed and Todd were probably together, but they're kids and unarmed."

"What did you want these for?" Claire Barndt asked, looking at the grocery sacks full of carrots Shigata had asked her to buy on the way in.

"I don't know," Shigata said. "Miner had bought carrots and Quinn had a hunch they were for a hippopotamus." He glanced, briefly, at Johnny Quinn. "I've learned to pay attention to Al's hunches. So first thing we're going to do at ArkPark is visit a hippopotamus."

Hansen rolled over, somewhat painfully, on what felt like damp concrete. His head hurt, he was hungry and thirsty, his bladder was full, and— "Hey, Quinn," he said, "what do you call a flower that has diarrhea all the time?"

"Danged if I know," Quinn replied, his voice a little slurred.

"A crapdragon," Hansen said. "Shigata's not going to like this," he added.

"I ain't too crazy about it myself," Quinn replied. He'd recognized Hansen only by voice, because it was certainly too dark to see anything. "How'd you know I was here?"

"I saw you when they brought me in. One of them had a flashlight. I think there's somebody else in here besides us, at least I heard somebody else moving around, but I don't know who."

"It's us." The voice was that of Ed Quinn.

"Oh, shit," Quinn said. "Both of you?"

"Yeah," Todd said.

"How'd that happen?" Hansen asked.

"We got a job here," Todd said, not fully coherently, "and we were supposed to start work tomorrow morning, I mean this morning—I guess it's morning because we've been here a long time, only you sure can't tell in here—and then they called and told us to go in last night. They told us to sort of walk around and look for anything that looked funny, and we did and we saw this door where there didn't ought to be a door and so we went in it." He seemed disinclined to explain further.

Ed picked up the story. "So somebody slugged us. We—I, anyway—woke up in I guess it was the middle of the night but, like Todd said, you sure can't tell by looking."

"Are both of you tied too?" Quinn asked.

"Yes," Ed said. "I'm sort of up against the edge of a piece of concrete here and it was pretty rough, so I was trying to rub the rope and fray it in two, but the rope must be real good, because all that happened is I've just about worn the concrete smooth."

"Keep trying," Quinn said.

"Okay," Ed said. "How'd they get you?"

"Somebody called my name, and I turned and somebody coldcocked me on the back of the head," Quinn answered. "Hansen, how about you?"

"Same as the kids. I tried to check out a door where one shouldn't be."

"Did they slug you too?"

"Yeah," Hansen said. "I feel like I've been pistol-whipped."

"You have a basis for comparison?" Quinn inquired, forgetting—as he sometimes did—his ignorant redneck role.

"I have a basis for comparison," Hansen replied grimly. "Another debt I owe that son of a bitch Dale Shipp."

"Forget about Dale Shipp," Quinn said. "Let's concentrate on getting out of here."

"Good idea," Hansen agreed. "You got any plans?"

Shigata was beginning to think that calling the Metro Intelligence Squad—or the Border Patrol—or the FBI—or any other agency he could think of, even if they did decide he was a flake, might be a better idea than trying to investigate a crime by feeding carrots to a hippopotamus.

You do not, he rapidly decided, hand-feed carrots to the hippo, even if the hippo does seem basically friendly, to say nothing of slothful. Its mouth was just too damn big and too damn full of teeth, many of which appeared to be about the size of the business end of a baseball bat. So he offered the first carrot to the hippo and then, when it showed interest, hastily dropped the carrot in front of it.

One question was immediately answered. Hippos do eat carrots. They probably don't eat them in the wild—Shigata rather doubted that carrots grow along the banks of the Nile or wherever it is that wild hippos still live, which come to think of it almost certainly is not in the Nile—but hippos in captivity eat carrots. They eat carrots with considerable relish and signs of pleasure and enthusiasm.

Shigata had seen hippos in zoos who seemed to spend their entire lives standing up, indoors, in concrete tanks no more than a foot or two longer and wider than they. This hippo—whatever its sex and name was; there was no informative notice—fared better. Its enclosure was both inside and outside, with a metal gate that could be closed if the weather got too inclement. Indoors, it could wade gradually into a tank that eventually got deep enough so it could submerge all except its nostrils and eyes, that being a pose hippos seem to like. Outdoors, it could lie down in a tank that contained not only water but also soft, squelchy mud.

At the moment, the hippo was inside. Not having any idea where Miner had wanted to lure the hippo from or to, if in fact that was the reason he had bought the carrots, Shigata was inside also, feeding carrots to the hippo in the hope that it would remain inside while Claire Barndt and Johnny Quinn searched the outside enclosure carefully for whatever they might find. It would have helped a lot if they'd had some idea what they were looking for.

Hippos can eat a lot of carrots very quickly, Shigata was discovering, and he was beginning to wonder whether he would have enough left to lure the hippo outside so that they could examine the inside of the enclosure.

Experimentally, he stopped offering them. The hippo made a noise that could, with very little imagination, be considered a sound of protest, and moved a step or two closer to Shigata. Shigata hastily moved a step or two back, tripped over a four-pound bag of carrots, and, before he could catch himself, fell into the tank with the hippo.

Ever since seeing *The Gods Must Be Crazy*, Shigata had wondered whether rhinos really stomp out campfires whenever they see them. He'd supposed it might be a useful adaptation in terms of protecting their territory from forest fires. But he had never before had occasion to wonder how a hippo would react if a police chief fell on top of it.

He didn't have time to wonder now. The hippo, quite as startled as the man, backed rapidly. Not having a carrot bag to trip over, it kept going, and as Shigata scrambled out of the tank, dripping extremely foul-smelling water, with a limp fragment of lettuce draped over his gun butt, the hippo exited to the exterior enclosure just as Barndt and Johnny came into the viewers' area inside.

"What the hell?" Johnny said.

"Never mind," Shigata answered. "Find anything?"

"Nary a nothing," Johnny said.

"Figures," Shigata said. "Look in here." He picked up the full carrot bags and headed outside, figuring he could at least dry off a little in the sun while continuing to offer carrots.

He wound up searching inside while Barndt fed the hippo

carrots. It wanted nothing more from Mark Shigata.

And they found nothing at all inside. Either they had all guessed wrong about Miner's intentions, or Miner had intended to lure some other animal, or Miner himself had been wrong and there was nothing here to find.

"What now?" Barndt asked.

"Now I do what I should have done in the first place," Shigata said. "I ask for help."

But, once back in the police station, he changed his mind again. "Thing is," he said to Johnny, "they think by now we're a bunch of bumbling incompetents. They've murdered two people under our noses, they've taken two police officers prisoner—"

"If they aren't dead too," Johnny said, his voice perfectly steady.

"They aren't," Shigata said. "If they were, we'd have found them. No, they're holding them for some reason, and the reason may well be a hostage bargaining chip. The way I see it, as long as it's just us prowling around—and my guess is they know all of us by sight now—they're not going to worry too much. If we go in with a bunch of federal agents—"

"They kill Dad," Johnny said. "And Ed. And Hansen. And Todd."

"That's what I'm afraid of," Shigata said. "So we've got to figure out some way to find them and get them back by ourselves. Ted, did you get anything?"

"I've got five gift shops and three boutiques that sell ivory," Barlow said. "They all say they're legal; they can show me certificates of origin proving the ivory was imported according to strict government regulations."

"Okay." Shigata looked at his watch. Eleven o'clock already; nobody had seen any of the four missing people in over sixteen hours. But he was still sure this was the best way to go about it. He'd been an FBI agent. He knew the Bureau's idea of doing things inconspicuously, and he wasn't going to trust Al Quinn's life—or Ed Quinn's, or Steve Hansen's, or even Todd Hansen's—to that. "Which malls?"

Barlow named four malls and a store on the Strand in Galveston. It would take a minimum of six hours for one man to hit them all.

But it was going to have to be done.

"Take a radio with you, but leave it in the car when you get in," he said. "Check them all. If you find one where the ivory matches the stuff from Ruskin, call me—no, don't use the radio, make it the landline. Call the office and have them give me a telephone number to call you on."

"If I find one, you want me to stop?"

"No," Shigata said, "check them all."

"Damn!" Hansen said explosively.

"What is it?" Quinn was instantly alert.

"I just wet my pants."

"Is that all?" Quinn said. "I did that two hours ago."

There was more silence, broken only by the very distant sounds of creaking and clanging, the much closer sound of water slowly dripping. "Is this a cave?" Todd asked.

"No, at least not a natural cave," Hansen answered. "You can't have a cave in this part of the country. The water table is too high. This is some kind of a construct. I'm glad you said something, though."

"Why?"

"You'd been quiet too long. I was beginning to worry."

"What's there to say?" Todd asked. "I'm thirsty. I'm scared. So is everybody else." There was a hint of a sob in his voice.

"And if you realize that," Quinn said softly, "you may be starting to grow up after all. Congratulations. May you live long enough to enjoy your newfound wisdom."

"Thanks," Todd said doubtfully.

"Hey, Quinn," Hansen said, "are you lying on the ground, or the floor, or whatever it is?"

"Yeah, why?"

"Well, I am too. And your hands are tied in back?"

"Yeah."

"Well, I got to thinking, maybe we could scoot close

enough together that I could untie your hands or you could untie mine."

"I tried that twenty-odd years ago," Quinn said. "It doesn't work. But you can try if you want to."

"Who tries to get to whom?"

"You've got to be the only guy in the universe who'd say 'whom' in a mess like this," Quinn said. "You got on long sleeves, or short?"

"Short, and I'm freezing my ass off. Why?"

"Mine are long," Quinn said. "Keep talking, I'll try to get to you."

"What difference does it make how long my sleeves are?"

"I can tell you never tried to scoot over concrete with your hands and feet tied."

"Oh. Yeah."

"I said keep talking."

Obediently, Hansen said, "Your talking about me saying 'whom' reminded me of this story I heard about a Harvard MBA. He knew everything about money, but he didn't know how to swim. So one day he fell in the river, and he started screaming, 'I am in dire need of assistance! I am in dire need of assistance!'" Hansen paused. "Not so good, huh?"

"Not so good," Quinn grunted. "Keep talking."

"Okay, well, one day a surgeon and an engineer and a lawyer got to talking about which one had the oldest profession. The surgeon said, 'When God created Adam he put him to sleep and removed one of his ribs to create Eve. That was clearly a surgical procedure, so that proves surgery is the oldest profession.'

"Then the engineer said, 'But wait a minute. Before that, God created the heavens and the earth out of chaos, and that clearly was a stupendous engineering feat. So engineering is the oldest profession.'

"And then the lawyer said, 'Now wait just a cotton-pickin' minute. Where do you think they got all that chaos?' Ow! Damn! That was my left hand, until your knee landed on it."

"It's still your left hand," Quinn growled. "Quitcher bitchin'. I found you, didn't I?"

"Yeah, you found me, and what happens next?"

"You're the guy with the bright idea, you figure it out."

Kids don't go to theme parks one person to a car—it's at least two, and sometimes six or eight or ten. But even so, it took an awful lot of cars to get 15,000 kids to ArkPark. Which meant it took an awful lot of time for Claire Barndt and Johnny Quinn to search the parking lot for the police car Al Quinn had driven, the small sedan Steve Hansen had driven, and the twenty-year-old pickup truck Ed Quinn had driven.

But all three were there. The police car was easiest to find, because it was parked along with no more than about twenty nonemergency vehicles in the "emergency vehicles only" area beside the front gate. Hansen's car, and Ed's pickup truck, were farther back, in general admission parking. All three were locked.

Meanwhile, Shigata went himself to check Hansen's house. As he had expected, no one was there. But he did find Todd's note.

"I don't care what time of day it is," Shigata said. "I don't care what time they got to bed. I want your chiefs of security up here, and I want them here now, or I go and get them."

Burton Wells and Glenn Wells, looking surprisingly alike, sat in the chairs in Shigata's office. "I don't know why you wanted us up here," Burton said.

"To ask you questions," Shigata said, acutely missing Quinn, who usually would be sitting at the side of the desk doing the bad-cop role while Shigata did the good-cop role. Now he'd have to play them both, and that would be enough to confuse a virtuoso actor. "Did Al Quinn go in last night to monitor the video screens?"

"He did not," Burton said promptly.

"But you didn't call the police station and ask where he was."

"No. Why should I? I just figured he changed his mind about coming in."

"What did you see on your video screens last night?"

"My security guards making their rounds," Burton said. "A chimpanzee having a baby. A bunch of animals doing their thing. Nothing else."

"Did you see Al Quinn or Steve Hansen?"

"I don't know what Al Quinn looks like," Burton said. "I don't even know who Steve Hansen is, though I suppose from your attitude he must be another cop."

Shigata tossed pictures on the desk, and Burton picked them up. "No, I didn't see either of them."

"You ever heard of Ed Quinn and Todd Hansen?"

"Yeah, they're those two kids Hobby hired. Like I need a couple of teenagers on my security staff. And if I did I'd hire them myself."

"Did you see them?"

"I've never met either of them," Burton said. "Anyway, do you know how many kids there were still there at ten o'clock? If I had seen them I wouldn't have noticed. Hell, I doubt I'd have noticed my *own* kids, in that crowd."

Shigata turned to Glenn Wells. "Did you see them?"

Glenn shook his head.

"They weren't scheduled to start work till Saturday," Shigata said. "Hobby called them and told them to come on in Friday night."

"He didn't tell me about it," Glenn said, "and he didn't tell them to report to me."

"How do you know he didn't tell them to report to you, if he didn't tell you about their coming in?"

"They didn't report to me, anyway," Glenn said.

The phone on Shigata's desk rang, and he reached for it. The dispatcher said, "Clifford Hobby's here and insists on seeing you now."

"Send him back," Shigata said.

"But I didn't tell them to come in Friday night," Hobby said. "I told them to come in Saturday morning, and that's the last I saw of them."

"And you didn't call Ed Quinn at home."

"I did not."

"His mother says you did, and she's not a woman given to lying."

"All the same, I did not. Friday night—Friday I left early. I had a meeting in Galveston, about the homeless shelter. I was there continually from five P.M. until nine P.M. Does that take in the time in question?"

"Will there be people to confirm that you were there?" Shigata asked hopelessly. Of course there would be, whether Hobby was there or not.

Hobby nodded. "The entire ministerial alliance of the city of Galveston."

And that meant Hobby was there. His secretary might lie for him; the inhabitants of his homeless shelter might lie for him. But it could be safely assumed that the entire ministerial alliance of the city of Galveston, taken in aggregate, would tell the truth about the presence on Friday night of Clifford Hobby.

So somebody else had called Ed Quinn.

But who? Nobody ought to have known he'd been hired, except Hobby's secretary and the Wells brothers.

"What's your secretary's name?" he asked.

"Evangeline Wells," Hobby said.

"Wells?"

"My wife," Glenn Wells explained.

"Any more questions?" Hobby asked.

Shigata shrugged. "No. Not now. You can go—all of you."

Three years ago, when he was in the Bureau, he could casually pick up a telephone and say, "I want a background check on Burton and Glenn Wells," and get one. It would be harder now. But one way or another he was going to get a background check on them, as well as on Clifford Hobby, and he was going to get it fast.

"Can you tell how it's coming?" Quinn asked. He'd been lying still, letting Hansen try to untie his bonds, and the circulation was partly cut off on his left side from the extreme awkwardness of the position.

"Just hold still, I've about got it."

"I can't hold still much longer," Quinn said. "Not if I expect to have an arm tomorrow."

"Try."

And, quite suddenly, the lights blazed on, and a voice said, "Very enterprising, Mr. Hansen. Very enterprising indeed. It appears that I got here just in time."

Hansen expected to see Clifford Hobby, when his eyes adjusted enough to see at all. But this was a man he'd never seen before in his life.

▽

Chapter 9

TEMPORARILY ALONE IN THE police station, waiting for reports from Ted Barlow, waiting for Johnny Quinn and Claire Barndt to get back from wherever they'd gone to eat whatever they'd gone to eat, Shigata picked up and opened the abandoned folder in which Hansen had been working out his theories. Besides neatly detailed pieces of reasoning and flowcharts that ran nowhere, there was a lot of doodling. One sheet of paper was headed "Dig at the center."

Obviously, that was part of Hansen's deconstruction theory. But Shigata wondered—what was the center?

In Hansen's reconstruction of the crime—the reconstruction he'd had to do on paper before getting to the deconstruction, also on paper—the center was a person, or a thing, or a fact, or a supposition. But what if the center was exactly that—a center? The center?

On the same sheet of paper, beneath Hansen's note to himself, Shigata began to sketch, drawing on his memories of ArkPark. Fifteen minutes later, he knew he was on the right track.

The alligator pit, the hippo enclosure, and the aquarium/diorama/seal tank area formed three corners of a square—a *large* square. Two of the corners—the aquarium area and the hippo enclosure—included both an interior, underground room for looking through glass, and an exterior, much higher, spot for looking directly down into the water; the third—the alligator pit—had a sunken area that could be viewed from ground level on two sides, or from a hill on the other two sides. The fourth corner of that square would be right at the edge of the park, beside the coast road. And the interior of the square formed a large artificial hill.

Furthermore, although the carefully planned layout of ArkPark prevented the casual visitor from noticing, the fourth corner of that artificial hill, the corner on the coast road, lay within 1,000 yards of the backside of Galveston Bay. Probably the pipes that brought saltwater into the aquarium and the seal tank ran that way. And where there were pipes, there could be a tunnel—even at this high water level—if engineering was adequate.

If the stakes were high enough, adequate engineering could be paid for.

Even accepting the need for machinery to keep water circulating and adequately filtered, water and air heated or cooled as need be, if that artificial hill was hollow, there would be probably 10,000 square feet of ground space available at the very least, and the concealed building would be at least one, probably two, possibly even three stories.

No, he wasn't absolutely certain that was where Margaret Ruskin had been shot, where Ralph Miner had been strangled, where somebody even now was holding Al Quinn and Ed Quinn and Steve Hansen and Todd Hansen, alive or dead. But he was sure enough to ask for a search warrant—if he had any idea how he could talk the judge into granting one.

When Quinn's eyes began to adjust to the blazing light, the first thing he saw was his son Ed, a long, deep laceration on his left wrist where he'd scraped it trying to rub the rope in two and stoically gone on scraping, standing with a chunk of cement in his hand. "Drop it," commanded one of the three armed men who'd come into the artificial cave.

Obediently, Ed dropped the rock and, without waiting for a command, dropped back down onto the damp floor, to sit and wait for orders. But there was a glint in his eye that told Quinn Ed had done what he meant to do; the chunk of concrete was only a smoke screen. When the man ordered Ed to his feet again, Quinn saw Ed's empty hip pocket. Unlike their captors, Quinn knew which pocket Ed carried his billfold in, and knew Ed always carried it.

When Shigata got there—if Shigata got there—he'd find the billfold. He'd know, from that, that he'd been on the right track so far. What good that would do depended on a lot of things, and how fast Shigata was was only one of those things.

Shigata snatched at the telephone, not knowing what—or who—he expected to hear at the other end. Ted Barlow's voice said, "Chief, I've got something. I don't know how much it's going to help."

"Give."

"I'm in Galveston, on the Strand. I just left this shop called Gulf and Pacifick." He spelled the last word and added, "Damned if I know why they spell it that way. It's like those ads in *Fate* where they spell magic with a *k* on the end. But it's real pricey, aimed at the rich tourist or upper-middle-class nouveau riche. I'm sorry, but I'm pretty sure they made me."

"Happens," Shigata said. "What were you able to get?"

"They have ivory—the bracelet, the hairpins, just like the ones Mrs. Ruskin had, and some other stuff too. One necklace made of little elephants holding each other's tails. Another thing they have—it's this miniskirt, and it's made of tiger fur. He tried to tell me it was really bunny fur, cleverly clipped and dyed. Chief, he was lying. I'm no furrier, but I know bunny fur when I see it, and that wasn't. Especially not with a twelve-hundred-dollar price tag on it, marked down today from only three thousand. The cheapest ivory set was five hundred, and they've got four boxes, four different sets, on display. The way the tiger skirt was cut, I figure they'd get four, maybe five skirts out of one pelt. I mean it was *real* mini, and no more than size five, more likely a three."

"Okay," Shigata said. Ted would know. He'd recently married, and his wife was about a size three.

"And boots of elephant hide, nine hundred dollars, men's size nine. They showed me provenance papers showing the ivory and elephant hide were legally imported. The papers were photocopies. I figure they imported one set legally and they're selling thirty or forty or more sets for each set of papers. Before they made me, I was asking questions about the store. This clerk or assistant manager or something was helping me, before the manager came and chased her away and took over. But the clerk, she told me Gulf and Pacifick is a chain. She said there are about thirteen hundred stores in the United States, mostly at high-class malls and resorts and places like that. You still want me to check those other stores on my list?"

"Never mind," Shigata said. "Head on in. When you get here, hold the fort. I'm heading back out to ArkPark."

But before he went, he grabbed his calculator. Thirteen hundred stores times over $500 in ivory plus thirteen hundred stores times a $1,200 skirt (marked down from $3,000, and how many would they sell at full price?) plus thirteen hundred stores times $900 for elephant hide boots times how many of these things would they sell in a given month, and what else would be available behind the counter for special customers—oh, yes, there was plenty of money there. Enough money to pay for ArkPark as a complicated cover. Enough money to pay for as complicated a piece of engineering as anybody would need.

For this, he definitely had to have a search warrant—if he could talk a judge into granting one. But most likely any judge would say, "This is all supposition on your part. You have no real probable cause." He'd get the warrant, one way or another, but it might takes days, and probably Quinn and Hansen, and their sons, didn't have days to wait. So maybe he could use strong-arm tactics and get by without a search warrant, and maybe he couldn't, but he was going to give it a shot. If he lost the case—cases—because of the strong-arm tactics, it might not matter so much, if he got his people

back alive. There'd be other ways, later, to get Clifford Hobby
or whoever in his organization was responsible—and Shigata
was beginning to have a pretty good idea who that might be.

Now that it was possible to see clearly, Quinn could tell that
they were in a very large underground room, all concrete and
steel. The dripping water he'd been hearing came from con-
densation on a pipe that ran to a pump, with some other
equipment. It was cold because air conditioning was running full blast. The most likely reason for that expense was
the bales that lay on shelving near six large industrial sewing
machines and some other stuff that looked like shoe repair
equipment, lasts and hammers and so forth. Quinn knew
what the bales were only because one of them was open.
That particular bale was leopard pelts; two of them were on
a cutting table. The other bales, apparently, were other animal pelts and animal hides.

The ivory, in another part of the room, was easier to recognize—whole tusks stacked like cords of firewood. Beside
the ivory was more equipment; it looked like saws and
presses of various kinds. Shelving contained rows of open
jewelry boxes, some already packed with ivory bracelets,
necklaces, and hairpins, some empty and waiting to be filled,
and rows of boot boxes that said they were Tony Lama but
Quinn knew they weren't, because Tony Lama boots aren't
made at a concealed location inside a hill at a theme park.

Conveyor belts led into the room from a tunnel beside the
water pipe and out of the room going up to another level.
This wasn't just a storage facility for smuggled goods; this
was a whole factory, unpopulated today, and why was that?
Because of the prisoners? Because of the murders that had
happened? He could see the spray of blood, bone, brain tissue
that undoubtedly marked the place Margaret Ruskin had
been shot; nobody had bothered to clean it up. Or was the
factory deserted today because of the murders that were
going to happen?

Quinn looked away from the facilities, back at his son. Ed
was lying where he'd fallen, after one of the men retied his

wrists, the ropes going over that long laceration, and then shoved him down. Ed was silent, but Quinn, whose ropes also had been retied roughly and tightly, was sure he was conscious.

He wanted to say something to Ed. But they wouldn't let him talk. And Ed would know what it was he wanted to say.

It wouldn't do any good for Hansen and me to beg them to let the boys go, he thought. They wouldn't do it. They're not going to let any of us live, not after we've seen this. I know that, Ed knows it, Hansen knows it, even Todd probably knows it. But for a wonder, even Todd was keeping his mouth shut.

After some deliberation, Shigata had sent Johnny Quinn—alone—down the coast road, to park the unmarked Bayport police car he was driving across the road from the nearest approach to ArkPark, and from there to walk through the brush and scrub down to the beach. "There'll almost certainly be a pump and a water inlet pipe down there. If there's anything else, it'll be nearby. Keep your eyes open for anything that happens, and guard your back," Shigata told him. "If you see anything—anything at all—radio me."

"Gotcha," Johnny said.

Shigata had taken Claire Barndt with him. Barndt had to be just about out on her feet by now, well over twenty-four hours awake and working, but she'd swallowed another cup of black coffee and announced herself ready to go.

He was prepared to shoulder his way past Hobby's secretary, into Hobby's private office, but Hobby's secretary wasn't there, and that tended to confirm a suspicion he'd found himself harboring. Hobby was in his office, and he looked startled, but not frightened, when Shigata strode in.

"Chief Shigata," he said, "I'm surprised to see you—but then this has been a day of surprises. Mrs. Wells did not appear, and now both Burton and Glenn seem to have taken off. While neither was scheduled to be on duty today, ah, still, I do expect—"

Shigata laid his rough map out on the desk. "What's here?" he demanded, ignoring Hobby's dithering.

Hobby looked down at the map.

"That hill?" he asked.

"Yes. That hill. What's in it?"

"That contains the facilities for—ah—for preparing food for the animals, and also the medical facility where we treat sick or injured animals as well as our first-aid facility for injured employees; the one for injured—ah—guests is, of course, more visible. We judged it best to conceal such facilities in order to preserve the theme of the park."

"Where do shipments come in? Food and medical supplies and so forth?"

"Right here." He pointed to the corner on the coast road. "There's a regular office area built into the wall that surrounds the park, and loading docks on the exterior."

"So boxes of animal food come in, and empty boxes go out."

"Well, yes, of course," Hobby said.

"So what if the outgoing boxes aren't empty?"

"Of course they're empty. They're sent out in bales for recycling, if they can't be reused directly. Chief Shigata, what—"

"That's the top level. What's in the level below that?"

"Storage facilities. We try to keep at least a week's supply of food on hand for all the animals, in case of—ah—transportation difficulties. Also, the water pumps and so forth and the—ah—air-conditioning machinery is there."

"And the level below that?"

"There isn't one. Chief Shigata, what—"

"Where did you get the money to build ArkPark?"

"I—ah—well, I had contributors, of course." Hobby peered at Barndt, as if she could—or would—protect him from this suddenly ferocious police chief. Barndt stared back at him, coolly.

"What kind of contributors? Private? Corporate?"

"I—ah—both, of course. Small private contributors, larger corporate contributors—some quite large, actually—"

"How much of a contribution did Gulf and Pacifick Corporation make?"

Hobby blinked. "Mr. Shigata, I'm afraid that's confidential—"

"The hell it's confidential," Shigata said. "Get this straight, Hobby. I have four people—two policemen and two teenage boys—missing at ArkPark. I'm convinced I know who put them there and why, and I'm going to get them out if I have to bring in a bulldozer and raze this whole park of yours. Now, answer my question. How much of a contribution did Gulf and Pacifick make?"

"Quite large," Hobby said. "They paid, ah, actually, half the expense of building the park, and they're paying half the expense of running it. Mr. Shigata, what do you mean, four people missing? Not those teenage boys I hired yesterday? Surely not—"

"When you hired the Wells brothers, did you go to them, or did they come to you?"

"Well—ah—actually, they came to me, and offered to plan and set up all necessary security matters for a percentage of the profits as well as a small salary. It was quite a good offer, as I am afraid I am not at all security minded myself."

The shape of the situation was exactly what Shigata had begun to suspect it was going to be. One more question, and he'd be sure. "Is Junior Athanasopoulous on your security staff? Or does he shovel hippo poop?"

Hobby blinked again. "Ah—I'm afraid I don't recognize the name."

"George Athanasopoulous, Junior. Check your personnel files, man."

Hobby toddled out to his secretary's office and opened a file drawer. "How do you spell that name again?"

Shigata spelled the last name.

"No," Hobby said, "there's no one by that name—or anything like it—employed at ArkPark."

"I thought there might not be." Shigata was feeling the warmth of satisfaction; now he knew who was responsible for the killings, for the kidnappings, for the smuggling Margaret Ruskin had found out about. Now all he had to do was get his people back, and call the Border Patrol and so forth in on an already cleared case. "Lead me to the inside of that hill—through that hidden door by the hippo enclosure." That was a long shot. There might not be a hidden door by the hippo enclosure, or if there was Hobby might not know about it.

But he did, because he didn't look startled at all. "Mr. Shigata, surely—"

"Are you going to lead me into your animal food facility, or am I going to call for the bulldozers?"

"Well—ah—you really needn't threaten me, Mr. Shigata, I'm quite willing—"

"I'm sure you are. So let's go."

"I know who you are," Ed Quinn said, looking up from his sprawl on the floor.

"Do you now," Burton Wells drawled. "Then that's one more nail in your coffin. Who am I?"

"You're Burton Wells. You're head of security at ArkPark. I saw your picture in that room with all the monitors. Yours too," he said to Glenn Wells. "And you—" He looked at Junior Athanasopoulous with loathing in his face. "I met you at a party at my brother's house. You kept watching his wife. I couldn't figure out which you were coveting, Mei Ling or Mei Ling's jewelry. I guess now I know. It was both."

"You've said enough," Burton snapped.

"You stole Mei Ling's jewelry to use as patterns for the ivory here," Ed continued. "Who made you give it back?"

"Him," Junior said sulkily, nodding at Burton. "He didn't want anybody to know it was gone. I'd have kept it, just like I'll keep her, one day when I get her, as long as I want to."

"And you stole new jewelry from here. That's what Mrs. Ruskin recognized when she was in your room. It matched the jewelry she'd already bought at Gulf and Pacifick. That's what started her thinking about ArkPark as a smugglers' nest. She knew where you worked."

Burton did a double take and took three steps toward Junior, fast. *"You did what?"*

"He's lying," Junior squealed. "I didn't—"

"Then how do I know what it looks like?" Ed demanded. "I know because I saw it." That was a bluff; he'd seen it, but not in Junior's possession. To Junior, he went on, "You've got a decent mother. I've met her, too. She'd really be proud of you if she could see you now, wouldn't she? And your dad—I haven't met him, but I've heard he's a decent, hardworking—"

"Shut up," Burton said. "You too, Junior. We'll discuss this later. I told you what to do, now do it."

Junior Athanasopoulous picked up a large knife from the cutting table and approached Ed. "No, the other boy," Burton ordered.

Todd watched his approach, his face white with terror, but evidently he was determined to follow the lead of Ed and of the adults. He was silent. But Junior only slashed the ropes at Todd's feet. "On your feet," he said.

It was hard to get up with his hands tied behind his back. But Todd managed.

"Now," Burton said, "the rest of you are going to do exactly what I say, or this kid dies first. Junior—"

Junior cut the ropes from Ed's feet, then from Hansen's, then from Quinn's. He backed off fast, before Quinn had time to get to his feet, and looked back at Burton for instructions.

"This is the order we're going in," Burton said. "Glenn'll go first, lead the way. Hansen behind him. Then Ed Quinn. Then Al Quinn. Then Todd and me'll be last, and Todd'll have a gun at his ribs the whole time, so if anybody acts up—"

"We hear you," Quinn said roughly. "Shut up before you scare the boy so bad he can't walk."

"Oh, he'll walk," Burton said softly. "He'll walk. See, I don't have to shoot to kill at first."

"Leave him alone!" Hansen yelled. "You want a hostage, take me, not him!"

"That's why we're taking him." Burton said, his voice silky with satisfaction that he'd finally drawn a response. "Because you don't want us to. But don't worry, you're all hostages, for just as long as we need you."

"And then you deep-six us," Quinn said, his eyes again on his son. Ed stared back, his courageous facade holding.

"And then we deep-six you," Burton agreed. "Now, move it."

"Why should we?" Ed demanded. "You're going to kill us all anyway, so why should we do anything you say?"

"Because," Burton said, "you all hope that if we let you live another half hour, you'll figure a way out of this."

"And maybe we're right," Quinn challenged.

"And maybe you're not," Glenn replied. Grinning, he motioned with the barrel of his pistol. "Thataway. Move it."

Single file, they went into the tunnel beside the water pipe.

The stretch of beach was absolutely deserted. All Johnny could see were the pump and intake pipe—Shigata had called that one right—and a distant boathouse. He walked aimlessly up and down the beach, not sure why he was there, but he knew his dad trusted Shigata, and right now his dad's life was at risk. Johnny had to let Shigata give the orders. That meant he had to take the orders, and carry them out the best he could.

But guard his back? You can guard your back if you've got a tree or a building to back up to, but how do you guard your back in a wide open area with no partner?

He kicked at a plastic milk bottle that had drifted up in a wad of seaweed, stopped once to pull out his pocketknife and methodically cut all the plastic rings in a six-pack holder, so that no sea animal or bird would get its neck tangled in it and strangle, picked up a long strand of abandoned fishing line and coiled it up and put it in his pocket for no particular reason except that he never left fishing line on the beach, and wished again that he knew what he was doing.

Anyhow, he was looking the right way when the small boat came out of the boathouse. It was an outboard motor boat, the kind that's often a dinghy for a yacht, and there were seven people in it. A name was painted on it in large letters—PACIFICKA, which was a little odd for Galveston Bay in the Gulf of Mexico in the Atlantic Ocean. Somewhere out there, he surmised, was a yacht named *Pacificka*.

He'd have noticed the boat even if he wasn't out here specifically to watch, because it was odd to see an occupied boat come out of a boathouse when nobody had gone in. He wasn't close enough to see faces, but even from this distance he could recognize his dad's and brother's posture, but oddly distorted, as if—as if their hands were tied behind their backs.

He ran toward the boat, but somebody revved the motor and the boat was gone, out of anything but bullet range, and he darn sure wasn't going to shoot at a moving boat that had his father in it.

He raised the radio in his hand and said, "Car One."

No answer.

He tried again.

"Car One. Do you copy?"

Still no answer.

He couldn't just stand here on the beach and wait, so what should he do?

He headed for the boathouse.

The top level inside the hill had been exactly what it was supposed to be. Kitchens, and Shigata was surprised at how sanitary the space was where the food was prepared, to be taken and dumped onto concrete floors or into rarely washed feeding bowls. A small animal hospital, which at the moment contained one very small chimpanzee in a diaper. A small clinic for humans, now containing one nurse who was reading the Houston paper.

Hobby led Shigata and Barndt down to the next level, which again was exactly what it was supposed to be. A few sides of beef or what looked like horse meat for the few predators in the park, a lot of lettuce and cabbage and carrots. "And this is it," Hobby said helplessly. "Chief Shigata, I can't help what you think, but there really is not another level."

Shigata grabbed an Arab-looking man who was wielding a meat cleaver. "Hey, man," he said, "how do I get down to the bottom level?"

The man looked at him blankly and pulled his arm away.

"He's Palestinian Arab," Hobby said. "He doesn't speak much English. I don't know why Burton wanted to hire so many Arabs, but—"

"Don't you?" Shigata said. "Then you're awfully stupid. It's because they don't speak English, of course." He grabbed a second man, repeated the question.

That man, too, stared at him blankly.

But a third man, one he had not addressed, said, "Stairs over there." He pointed at a corner.

It was that easy.

All the way down the stairs, Hobby kept saying, "I didn't know—there isn't supposed to be—" At the bottom of the stairs, he looked around in what Shigata would have been willing to swear was honest bewilderment. "But I don't understand—"

Then he caught sight of the pelts, the hides, the ivory. He walked over to them, and Shigata realized, in some astonishment, that Hobby was crying. "But this is the Ark," he was saying. "This is the Ark. I meant to save animals—to teach people that God wants them to save the animals. I don't understand—"

"You've been had," Shigata said softly. "You've been used."

"Chief," Barndt called, from the other side of the vast underground room.

Shigata turned. "What have you got?"

"Ed Quinn's billfold, and some blood beside it."

"How much?" Shigata asked quickly.

"Not that much." She knew what he was asking. "Like somebody got a little bit of a cut. That's all. And there's some cut rope over here. Four sets. And Steve's police radio."

Johnny needed to know this. But when Shigata tried to use his radio, he realized no signal was getting in or out through the earth, metal, and concrete that surrounded him.

Johnny would have been willing to bet that whatever door led into the boathouse from outside, the entrance they had used to get to the boat without being seen would be locked. He'd have bet wrong. Apparently, arrogantly, they'd counted on nobody ever entering the boathouse. The door was metal, solidly built to hold back even the storm surge from a hurricane, and it led into an equally solid tunnel or series of caissons, dim with electrical lights at slightly too wide intervals.

Anybody who goes into a tunnel by himself, not knowing what's at the other end, without anybody knowing he's going there, is a damn fool, Johnny told himself. But right now, with his dad's life at stake, he was willing to be a damn fool. Only he took his pistol out of his holster, held it at arm's length, led with it.

And he heard movement ahead, somebody walking. "Freeze!" he yelled.

A moment of silence, then Shigata's voice. "Johnny? That you?"

"Yes—I saw Dad. And the others."

"Where?" Shigata was coming toward him. "How'd you get in here?"

"Dad was in a boat. The others too—Ed, and Mr. Hansen, and Todd. This tunnel leads to a boathouse. They're taking them out to sea. We've got to—"

It was time, now, to call the Coast Guard, to call the Border Patrol. Shigata used the telephone on the wall beside the bank of sewing machines. And a bored voice at the other end said, "Let me call you back. Bayport Police Station?"

"I'm not there now. I'm at ArkPark, and I can't find the extension number I'm calling from."

"I'll call your dispatcher, then."

"My radio won't transmit from here. My dispatcher won't know what's going on. Give me five minutes to call—"

"Right," the bored voice said. "You're the Bayport chief of police and you're calling from ArkPark and your dispatcher doesn't know what's going on but you want us to go out and board a yacht without even having a search warrant. Right. Hey, buddy, we don't have time to play games, okay?"

Shigata hung up, numbly, and dialed again, this time the Galveston County Sheriff's Office. If he could get a dispatcher he knew, one who'd recognize his voice—but the voice that answered the telephone was absolutely unfamiliar to him. He hung up again, without even bothering to speak. Johnny, watching his face, said, "What—"

"We're on our own," Shigata said. "Can you find out if your uncle Hoa is in port?"

Johnny headed for the phone.

The boat was bouncing a little, and Quinn found himself slung against Ed's shoulder. Ed pushed back, bracing them both, until Quinn caught his balance again. "Ed?" Quinn said. "I'm sorry you're in this."

"I don't guess I was quite ready to be a cop yet," Ed returned.

"Give yourself time," Quinn advised, knowing perfectly well how inane that sounded under the circumstances.

After a moment, Ed replied, "Right." Quinn could hear a wry grin in his voice. After a moment Ed added, "Oh, well, it was interesting while it lasted."

"I got Uncle Hoa," Johnny reported. "He'll have the engine running, waiting for us."

"Give me the phone back," Shigata said. When he reached the dispatcher, he asked, "Is Ted Barlow back in? . . . Good, let me talk to him. . . . Ted, do you know the slip where Hoa's shrimp boat stays? Then meet us there, ten-thirty-nine. Have five shotguns with you and all the ammo you can carry . . . right."

Ten-eighteen is red lights and siren. Ten-thirty-nine is floorboard it. You don't run ten-thirty-nine very often, especially not in somebody else's territory.

But Johnny Quinn was a deputy sheriff. The whole state of Texas was his territory. And because of treaties made when Texas entered the United States, the territorial waters of the state of Texas extend clear out to the national limit.

If they could just get the yacht *Pacificka* before she got into international waters—

Of course Johnny Quinn might get fired from the job he'd

just been hired for yesterday, because he was acting without orders or authorization. But if he was, then Shigata had a slot he'd fit right into, and no more doubts about putting him in it.

"What's this boat you're talking about?" Hobby asked.

Shigata looked at him. "Why do you want to know?"

"I—have friends," Hobby said. "I might be able to get you some help."

This called for a quick decision, and Shigata made it. "The *Natalie*," he said. "A bright blue shrimp boat. The boat we're going after is the *Pacificka*. I figure she's a yacht. And I figure your security people are on her."

Shigata's marked car was at the main gate to the park. The car Johnny had driven was a lot closer. It was unmarked, but it had a siren, and a switch to turn the headlights so that they'd rapidly alternate, one light dim and one bright. Even in broad daylight, that would be noticed.

So how fast could three people—one of them nearly fifty, one of them almost asleep on her feet, one of them terrified that his father was going to be murdered before he could get there to stop it—run up three flights of stairs and out a door they didn't know the location of?

Shigata guessed they'd find out real quick.

$\triangledown$

Chapter 10

CLIFFORD HOBBY WAS PANTING, dripping with sweat, his natty gray suit half ruined, by the time he got back into this office. But his suit wasn't all that was half ruined. He was well aware that without the money from Gulf and Pacifick, he would probably lose ArkPark and everything else he had built up.

But knowing what he knew now, he couldn't continue to accept Gulf and Pacifick's money . . . if, indeed, Gulf and Pacifick had any money to offer him by the time this day was over.

And he hadn't been lying when he'd told Shigata he knew somebody who might be able to help. Any other Saturday afternoon he wouldn't have had the faintest idea where to locate Chaplain Bruce Talmadge, commander, United States Coast Guard. But this one Saturday afternoon he did know. Very nearly the entire Galveston County Ministerial Alliance was on the charter fishing boat *Kingfisher*. Hobby had bowed out of the trip for an ignominious reason: He got seasick. That was why his ark had to be on land.

But it was highly unlikely that Chaplain Talmadge would be seasick. If he could reach him, ship-to-shore phone—

Ship-to-shore phone had one disadvantage. Anybody with the right equipment could listen in and hear everything he had to say, everything Talmadge would shortly have to say to other people. But that couldn't be helped now.

It took him some time to get across to Talmadge just what the problem was. He wasn't a good extemporaneous speaker, and for something like this he couldn't take the time to write a script.

But finally he was assured that Talmadge knew the shrimp boat *Natalie* needed help and the yacht *Pacificka* and its dinghy had to be stopped, and that Talmadge would see to it the Coast Guard was duly notified.

The next telephone call he made was to the Border Patrol. No matter what honesty cost him—and this time it wouldn't cost him anything he wouldn't have already paid—he wanted those pelts, those skins, those tusks out of ArkPark as fast as possible.

And maybe the Border Patrol would like to be in on the chase.

Climbing out of a bouncing dinghy, onto the deck of a yacht, with bound hands wasn't the easiest task in the world. But eventually all four managed it, with the somewhat unwilling help fore and aft of both Wells brothers and Junior Athanasopoulous. Quinn considered kicking whoever was behind him—probably Glenn Wells—in the face but refrained on the ground that such an action would get him nothing but another pistol whipping, and he was still hurting from the first.

All four were ushered into the presence of an extremely elegant man in an extremely elegant stateroom. The man— fairly young (mid to late thirties), brown hair, blue eyes, with a somewhat petulant look—glared at Burton Wells. "You've made some serious mistakes," he said.

"Yes, sir, I—"

The man fixed his eyes on the Hansens, the Quinns, as if they were representatives of a particularly obnoxious breed of insect. "Who are these?" Then he stiffened, sat up straight. "*Cops?* You damn fool—"

"We had to," Burton shouted despairingly. "We were making a shipment last night—it was supposed to be safe, the cop was supposed to be in the guardroom with *us*, for cryin' out loud—and the monitor wasn't on there, so I didn't know—and those damn fool Ay-rabs had the door open, and everybody kept walking in—"

"So you—"

"I wasn't even *there*! It was that stupid kid, Junior—he couldn't think of nothing better to do than knock them out and tie them up, and I didn't even find out till the next morning—I told you we had to!" Burton shouted. "It was that or kill them there, and—we could have got away with the woman, and that other guy, but cops—I figured we could bring them out here and deep-six them and then nobody'd ever know—"

"And what would you suggest we do with them in the meantime?" the man asked, his voice heavy with sarcasm.

"Well—uh—hostages, maybe. Hostages, sir."

"Hostages." He continued to stare. "Well, I suppose we may need hostages. But we wouldn't if you hadn't been so foolish. You have set my work back ten years, and none of it was necessary. Alligators, indeed!"

"We thought—"

"Never mind what you thought. You may consider yourselves very fortunate that I still have a use for you. Which one of you was it who killed that harmless fool of a conservationist?"

A brief silence, during which the Wells brothers looked at each other. Finally, Glenn said reluctantly, "Me."

"I should have known. You're the practical joker. Did you kill that woman, too?"

"No, that was Burton."

"But you thought of the alligators, I suppose?"

"Well—"

"And gave them her purse as well, so they'd know exactly who she was?"

"I didn't mean to," Glenn yelled. "It slipped!"

"And the ivory slipped into it, I suppose?" Glenn didn't answer, and the man repeated, "I should have known it was

you. Nobody else would be that stupid. But we'll discuss this
further at a later date. Did you get me her journal?"

"Yes, sir." Obviously glad he'd done something right, Burton laid a brown vinyl folder on the table beside the man. "If
I hadn't seen her writing in it—"

"Right, right," the man said. "But who got her interested
in ArkPark to start with?"

"That was Junior—"

"Junior again? And who hired Junior? I repeat: you may
consider yourselves fortunate—all of you—for now. Glenn,
take those three below." He gestured to both Quinns, Steve
Hansen. "This one"—he looked at Todd Hansen—"we'll
keep in here."

"Let him go," Steve Hansen said. "Use me for whatever—"

"There is no need for histrionics," the man said. "You'll
all wind up in the same place quite soon. Glenn, if you
please—get them out of here. They stink."

"You would too if you'd been tied up without a bathroom
or any water!" Todd yelled.

"Hold your tongue, unless you wish to be gagged," the
man said coldly. "Homer!"

Another man—presumably Homer—entered. "Yes, sir?"

"Have you been monitoring ship to shore?"

"No, sir. Should I do so?"

"You might well do so for a time. Have you been monitoring Coast Guard frequencies?"

"Yes, sir."

"Any unusual activity?"

"None, sir. Some maneuvers going on. One cutter has
been ordered to intercept a shrimp boat and check for unusual activity."

"What's the shrimp boat's name?"

"*Natalie*, sir."

"Are we acquainted with *Natalie*?"

"No, sir."

"Very well. Carry on."

Both Quinns managed to keep their faces impassive, and
probably neither Hansen remembered at the moment who

Natalie belonged to. But the situation no longer seemed irrevocably lost.

Only almost lost, Al Quinn thought. Because the Coast Guard didn't know where either *Natalie* or *Pacificka* was, and *Natalie* didn't know where *Pacificka* was. And the Gulf of Mexico is a much larger body of water than one would think just from looking on a map.

Shigata, of course, had no idea that the Coast Guard had been notified. As far as he knew, he and his pitifully small team had to take *Pacificka* alone, and that—considering that *Pacificka* was undoubtedly larger, probably better armed, and certainly had hostages—was not going to be a simple chore.

He'd left Hoa to work on locating *Pacificka*, because the Gulf was what Hoa knew as well as Shigata knew the law and the land. He hadn't the slightest idea how Hoa was going about the task. But Hoa's brother-in-law and nephew were on *Pacificka*, and Hoa would do everything he could to get them back. Shigata was busy issuing shotguns and making sure they were loaded. Ted Barlow, Claire Barndt, Johnny Quinn, Rene Hoa (who wasn't old enough to deputize, but Shigata wasn't going to have anybody on board unarmed), and himself—Shigata didn't need to arm Captain Hoa. He'd bought a pistol, a rifle, and a shotgun the day after he got his citizenship papers, on the ground that he had lost one country to communism and didn't intend to lose another. All those weapons were on board.

Rene, leaving his just-issued shotgun on deck, climbed up on top of the boom for the trawl and sat straddling it, occasionally climbing around to get views of different parts of the horizon. Two or three times he shouted, in Vietnamese, to Hoa, and each time Hoa changed course.

After the fourth course change, Rene climbed back down off the boom and picked up the shotgun. "*Pacificka*'s over there," he told Shigata. "We'll see her in about five minutes."

He was as good as his word.

"How'd you do that?" Shigata asked.

Rene shrugged. "No big deal. I saw her about there yesterday, spearfishing. I didn't figure she'd have gone too far, not if she was still unloading contraband, like you told Dad."

But the next question was, were the four really on board, and, if so, what could Shigata do about it? It seemed very unlikely that *Pacificka* could be boarded. Shigata had never engaged in a sea fight, and never expected to. He found himself wondering what Quinn would do if the situation were reversed, and then, feeling like a complete jackass but pretty sure he was using correct terminology, he shouted, "Ahoy, *Pacificka*!"

"What is it?" somebody shouted back from *Pacificka*. "Back off, *Natalie*, we've been out here skin-diving and spearfishing and we're preparing to get under way."

"*Pacificka*, I'm Police Chief Mark Shigata of Bayport, and—"

"I'm Captain Roger Catton, and you're out of your jurisdiction."

"And this is Deputy Sheriff Johnny Quinn," Shigata went on, ignoring the interruption. "You are in Texas territorial waters. Deputy Quinn's jurisdiction extends over the entire state of Texas, and the rest of us are assisting him. We have reason to believe there is contraband on board your ship. Stand by to be boarded."

"You got a search warrant?"

"We don't need one. A ship is extremely portable. All we need is probable cause."

Catton made a biological, and quite impossible, suggestion about what Shigata could do with his probable cause, and then yelled, "Junior! Get up here, with the kid."

In a moment, one of Shigata's questions was answered. Junior—whoever Junior was, and Johnny explained that a few moments later—came on board with Todd Hansen and a pistol. "Now back off," Catton ordered. "We don't mind killing this one. We've got three more. Back off. We're moving out."

There is a story about a woman who went and camped by the gates of a vast city with nine books, which she said contained all the wisdom in the world. She offered to sell them for a vast sum of gold. The city fathers refused. Unper-

turbed, she burned three of the books, then went away. She came back the next year, offering the remaining six books for the same price she'd asked before, and again the city fathers hooted at her. She burned three more of the books and went away again. But when she sat down to light her fire with the three remaining books of wisdom, the city fathers pleaded wit her to wait. This time, they would buy the books. And they wound up paying for them the same price she had asked at first for all nine of the books.

The volumes were the Sibylline oracles.

Theoretically you don't bargain with those who hold hostages. Theoretically you keep them talking and give them very small things—a sandwich, a newspaper, radio time— but never anything big, no matter what happens to the hostage. But these people didn't want a sandwich, a newspaper.

If Shigata let them kill Todd Hansen—and he knew he could never live with himself if he did—how much more would they ask for Steve Hansen alive? If he let them kill Steve Hansen, what about Ed Quinn? And, finally, what about Al Quinn? What would he give—honestly, what would he give to keep Al Quinn safe?

But if he gave them what they wanted—a free passage to international waters—they'd kill the hostages anyway.

Intellectually, he knew that.

But his stomach didn't.

"Let the boy go, Catton," he said hopelessly.

Johnny, watching, found his hands in his pockets, found himself clutching the fishline he'd picked up on the beach as if it were a lifeline. And maybe—maybe— He took the fishline out of his pocket, looked at it.

Heavy. He'd hate to try to guess how many pounds it would test. Shark line, it looked like.

Stuffed into a yacht's screw, it could foul the screw. But a man who tried to stuff fifteen yards of fishline into a yacht's screw was likely to lose his hand, if not his life. Still, if nobody did anything to stop the yacht, Johnny was going to lose his father and his brother.

He didn't tell anybody what he was trying to do, because

he knew anybody he told would try to stop him, and they would be right.

He stripped off his gun belt, his boots, stuck his wallet into one of his boots. He hesitated over his pocketknife; it was heavy, but he might need it. He put it back in his pocket. Then, still in his jeans and shirt, he dived overboard, on the far side of *Natalie,* where Catton and Junior wouldn't see him. Shigata turned just in time to see him cleave the water. But Shigata had sense enough not to yell.

Gulf Stream or no, this water was cold, and for a moment Johnny couldn't get his breath. But then the water began to feel warmer, and he was breathing again. With strong, steady strokes, he began to swim toward *Pacificka.*

Until something in the water caught his eye.

An impromptu meeting of the Galveston County Ministerial Alliance was held on board the *Kingfisher;* at its conclusion Talmadge, who had been appointed temporary spokesman, approached the captain. "You're crazy," Captain David Rubacava said, after listening for two minutes.

"We're all in agreement."

"You realize that if that son of a—'scuse me, padre—if that yacht rams us we'll sink?"

"We're all in agreement," Talmadge repeated, mentally agreeing that Rubacava was undoubtedly correct. He added, "Saint Paul was shipwrecked several times. We're certainly no more important than he was. I repeat, we want you to locate *Pacificka* and place this boat between *Pacificka* and the open sea."

"You're crazy," Rubacava said again. But then he said, "Four hostages? Two of them kids?"

"That's right," Talmadge said.

Rubacava turned to his first mate and asked, "Where was *Pacificka* lying when we saw her yesterday?"

People who saw Todd Hansen and didn't know him tended to think that because he was fat he was helpless. He wasn't. One thing he was good at was a game called hackeysack, which involves keeping a small beanbag aloft with one's feet . . . and anybody who can play hackeysack well can kick just about anything.

Another thing he was good at was swimming.

He wouldn't have fought Burton Wells, because he was too afraid of Burton Wells. But Junior Athanasopoulous was another matter. Junior wasn't much older than he was, and Junior was slouched by the railing on Todd's right, holding the gun almost but not quite on the right side of Todd's rib cage. The barrel was pointing very slightly away, down, toward the water.

Without taking the deep breath that might alert Junior that something was going on, Todd kicked out quite suddenly, first catching Junior in the kneecap and then in the hand that held the pistol. He would have grabbed on to it, not that he was quite sure what he could do with it against that many other armed men, but with his hands bound that was impossible, and the pistol splashed into the Gulf of Mexico. Todd kicked Junior again, this time in the groin, and without a second's hesitation Todd followed the pistol into the Gulf.

His hands were still tied behind him, but he was making halfway decent progress just kicking his feet in the water, except that his body weight was distributed wrong and he kept swallowing water and choking.

Captain Catton was shooting at him, but Todd was bobbing in the waves, and his head was a small target. Then someone grabbed him, and he struggled wildly, and Johnny Quinn said, "Don't fight me."

"What are you doing here?" Todd panted, without noticing that the shooting had stopped.

"Never mind that," Johnny said. "Just don't fight me." He towed Todd over to *Natalie* and lifted him up, and other hands pulled him, gasping and sputtering, into the boat. Todd didn't even know who was cutting the ropes on his wrists; he was busy looking at Shigata, saying, "They've got my dad. And Mr. Quinn, and Ed— Say, what are you doing here, anyway?"

"Mounting a rescue," Shigata answered gravely. "Why don't you go on below and get something to drink?"

There was more commotion on *Pacificka*. In sheer disbelief, Shigata realized that *Kingfisher*, which he knew well from past fishing trips, had dropped anchor directly forward of *Pacificka*. "*Kingfisher*, move out," Catton shouted.

"Sorry," Rubacava shouted back. "This is where my passengers want to fish."

And that, Shigata saw in even more disbelief, was exactly what *Kingfisher*'s passengers were doing, crowding over the rails and casting into the water.

"*Kingfisher*, if you don't move out I'm going to ram you," Catton shouted.

"My passengers told me not to move," Rubacava returned. "Are we playing chicken?"

Johnny, astern of *Pacificka*, heard none of this. He was swimming around the screw, which was very slightly forward of the stern in a sort of alcove so that it could be approached from the sea.

For a wonder, the screw was completely still, although the engines were humming and *Pacificka* had begun to weigh anchor. Taking a deep breath and then diving, Johnny swam as close to the screw as he dared and began very artistically weaving the fishline in among the screw's blades, estimating where to put the line to do maximum damage. He didn't hear Catton yelling, "Full speed ahead," but something, a change in the sound of the engine, alerted him, and he backed water, grabbing hold of barnacles on the extreme aft of the hull of *Pacificka*, feeling them cut his hand and hoping they were fixed firmly enough, and he could hold on firmly enough, to keep from being drawn into the screw. He hoped, furthermore, that this wouldn't be the moment a shark picked to turn up, because blood from his hands was visibly coloring the water. And he hoped the screw would stop fast, because sooner or later he'd have to breathe again.

But he had to fight the current only for a moment, before

a horrible whanging sound came from the screw. He hadn't totally disabled it, but he'd yanked it very badly out of line. "We're fouled on something," he heard somebody shout.

"Reverse engines one-quarter," Catton ordered.

The engines reversed; now the current from the screw was thrusting Johnny away instead of pulling him in. As he surfaced, breathing hard, the horrible noise continued. *Pacificka* wasn't going anywhere, at least not very fast, until somebody came overboard to untangle the fishline and realign the blades.

Hoping that everybody would be on the side of *Pacificka* that faced *Natalie*, Johnny swam slowly around the other side, looking at the portholes below the main deck but above the waterline.

"What happened?" Barndt asked Shigata. "That noise—"

"My guess is that Johnny succeeded in doing whatever he went there to do."

"I hope he's okay."

Shigata didn't answer. There didn't seem to be a whole lot to say.

For another miracle, the porthole was open. It was far too small for Johnny to get in, but he could get his pocketknife in. He tapped very softly on the metal. Quinn turned quickly and then rose and walked toward the porthole. He turned when he reached it, to let Johnny put the open knife into his hands. The stretch was just a little too far for Johnny to cut the ropes himself, but with three of them in there . . . "Todd's safe," Johnny whispered. "He's on *Natalie*. I'm going to see what else I can do here."

"Take care," Quinn returned.

"I will."

He swam on around to the anchor chain, which was still only half raised, and climbed up it.

From *Natalie*, Shigata could see Johnny move quietly around behind Captain Catton and grab suddenly, the inside of his left elbow around Catton's neck, snatching Catton's pistol with his right hand. Seeing Junior approaching Johnny from behind, Shigata tried to shout a warning, but before he had his mouth more than open, Junior had slammed something—Shigata couldn't tell what—down onto Johnny's head, and Johnny slumped to the deck.

They were almost back to where they had been to start with. *Pacificka* had four hostages. But *Natalie* had exchanged Johnny Quinn, who was considerably useful, for Todd Hansen, who was of no conceivable use. Shigata hoped *Pacificka*'s engines were sufficiently disabled to make up for the loss, but he didn't want to gamble on it.

Both Quinns and Steve Hansen were untied now, but they were still inside a locked cabin. Al Quinn was attempting to pick the lock with the blade of the pocketknife, but his hands were half numb from being bound too tightly, and he was making poor headway.

They could all hear yelling on the deck. Then Catton's voice, very clearly, shouted, "Hey, Police Chief Mark Shigata! We've got your deputy sheriff over here."

He couldn't hear Shigata's reply, because just then the lock gave and the door swung open. Quinn almost, but not quite, toppled on his face.

But then he was on his feet again. They had to be careful—very careful indeed—because there were fewer of them, because they were unarmed and the crew of *Pacificka* was armed, because Johnny now was captive.

If *Pacificka* really had been spearfishing—and probably somebody had, if that was the cover story—then there ought to be a spear gun somewhere, probably several. If they could find them—

They fanned out, barefoot, walking as quietly as possible. It was Quinn who found the locker, its door partly open, that had the spear guns in it. He took two, made sure they were loaded. Then, with one held at ready and one under his left arm, he started—still as quietly as possible—for the cabin, where the young man who presumably was the boss of the operation sat.

He didn't try to go through the ship. He went outside, slipped around on the side of the deck that was away from *Natalie*, gambling—as Johnny had done—that everybody's attention was focused on *Natalie* or *Kingfisher*.

But nobody can have all the luck. Although the man was facing away from Quinn, in his big armchair, the porthole was locked. And even a spear gun isn't much use against a porthole cover meant to withstand gale-force winds.

That meant he had to get back off deck and find his way to the stateroom through the passageways. He wasn't sure he could do it. Especially without being spotted.

Johnny was unconscious, lying on the deck. Junior Athanasopoulous, murder on his face, was standing over him with another pistol, clearly restrained from killing only by somebody else's orders.

"Who's the best shot among us?" Shigata asked quietly. "I fired an eighty-seven last time I went to the range. I hope somebody's better than me."

"Ninety-two," Barlow said. "I'm not much better."

"I fired ninety-eight," Barndt said.

Shigata turned to look at her. "Do you mind killing somebody?"

"Not if I have to."

"Hoa, let her have your rifle," Shigata said, and Hoa silently handed the rifle over, accepting Barndt's shotgun in return.

"Now climb up there on top of the cabin and lie down, where he can't see you. If you have to fire, take that kid out first, the one with the pistol on Johnny."

"Right," Barndt said. She handed the rifle to Shigata and began to climb, on the far side of *Natalie* from *Pacificka*. Moments later Shigata handed the rifle up to her. Then he turned. "Catton!" he shouted.

"What is it?"

"We've got a sharpshooter in place. Surrender or die."

"You're lying," Catton shouted. "I know how many men you had. We've got one of them now, and you've got all the others with you. All you've got off deck right now is that foxy blond. Don't try to convince me that fat kid we had over here is a sharpshooter."

"I wouldn't dream of it," Shigata returned. "The sharpshooter is that foxy blond."

"Homer!" Catton shouted. "Bring up the other kid. We're going to waste this one."

"Claire," Shigata said quietly, and heard the rifle crack over his head.

Junior fell, the pistol scudding from his hand across the deck, and Catton gaped in utter disbelief before raising his own pistol.

Quinn heard the crack of rifle fire from *Natalie,* first one shot, then a pause and a second shot. He was almost to the stateroom now, close enough that when the man stood up and headed for the door Quinn was able to take two more steps forward and place the spear gun at the man's stomach. "Keep walking," he invited.

The invitation was declined.

"Then call off your dogs," Quinn said.

The man gulped and then shouted, "Catton!"

"I think Catton's dead," somebody answered from deck.

"Homer? Is that you?"

"Yeah, but—uh—"

"He's not going anywhere," another voice said. And Quinn rejoiced. That was Hansen.

When they'd taken Quinn's pistol, while he was unconscious in ArkPark, they had—for reasons he couldn't begin to imagine—left his handcuffs. He used them now and propelled the man ahead of him onto the deck.

He could see that Junior would probably live to stand trial; Catton almost certainly wouldn't. Johnny was sitting up, rubbing his head; Steve Hansen and Ed Quinn were holding

Homer and five other crewmen at bay with spear guns. Obviously they, too, had found the locker.

Continuing to propel the man ahead of him, Quinn stepped to the deck. "Hey, Chief!" he shouted. "We've got it under control over here!"

"Glad to see it," Shigata shouted back and turned to look at the Coast Guard cutter that was just moving into sight. "The cavalry's late again."

The Coast Guard had taken over *Pacificka*. Both Wells brothers were now in handcuffs, and, thanks to their highly opportune confession to Leon Aston—that turned out to be the name of *Pacificka*'s owner—they stood a good chance of conviction.

Margaret Ruskin's diary, which Burton Wells had killed her to get, was now in Shigata's possession, and he hoped it would give him a little better idea what had sent the councilwoman on her suicidal surveillance of ArkPark. Although there now seemed little doubt that she had found some of the smuggled ivory while cleaning Junior Athanasopoulous's room, that didn't seem sufficient cause to excite the suspicions of even a notoriously suspicious woman. Something else must have happened, and by the time the Wells brothers and Leon Aston went to trial, Shigata intended to know what it was.

Al Quinn, now on *Natalie*, was hugging Johnny and Ed at the same time, crying without any embarrassment. Quite suddenly, Shigata remembered Quinn, not too long after he and Quinn had met, saying to him, "Johnny, my oldest boy, well, we're not quite sure he's mine, you know what I mean. But he don't know. He never will know."

If he did know, Shigata realized now, it wouldn't matter.

Hansen was sitting on a coil of rope, one hand on Todd's arm, the other on Claire Barndt's. "You're still going, aren't you?" he asked her.

She nodded. "It's right for me. It might not be for you, but it is for me. I—I'm sorry. Sort of."

"Don't be," Hansen said. "I had a lot to get over. I'm not well yet, but I'm a lot better. You helped." He paused. "You've got something to get over now."

She shrugged. "I'll manage. Catton was starting to shoot at me, you know."

"Yes. I know." He turned his attention to Todd. "You thought pretty fast yourself, sport, once you got the chance."

Todd looked down at the deck, wriggled a little. "I just tried to think what you would do."

For the first time in his memory, Hansen was rendered altogether speechless.

In his office, Clifford Hobby was preparing the most important speech of his life.

If he could just convince the Galveston County Ministerial Alliance that it would be worthwhile for all the churches to work together to support ArkPark—